The Quest of the **Warrior SHEEP**

CHRISTINE & CHRISTOPHER RUSSELL

EGMONT

This book is dedicated to Gwen, June, Rachel and
Margaret, the Island Aunties.

EGMONT

We bring stories to life

The Quest of the Warrior Sheep
First published in Great Britain 2010
by Egmont UK Limited
239 Kensington High Street
London W8 6SA

Text copyright © Christine and Christopher Russell 2010
Cover illustration copyright © Colin Stimpson 2010

The moral rights of the author and cover illustrator have been
asserted

ISBN 978 1 4052 4376 6

3 5 7 9 10 8 6 4

A CIP catalogue record for this title is available from the British
Library

Typeset by Avon DataSet Ltd, Bidford on Avon, Warwickshire
Printed and bound in Great Britain by the CPI Group

Contents

1
The Baaton

All the sheep were chewing cud when it happened.

Actually, that's not quite true, because Oxo, the enormous Oxford ram, had finished chewing and was butting a fence post that had given him a funny look. Links, the Lincoln Longwool with floppy curls, was composing a rap. Jaycey, the pretty little Jacob, was painting her hooves with mud and sheep-dip. And Wills, the orphaned Welsh Balwen lamb, was wishing he was at football practice.

In fact, of the five Rare Breed Sheep in Ida White's field in Eppingham, only Sal, the Southdown with a wide bottom and thin legs, was really chewing cud. She was sitting digesting yesterday's grass, passing it from one stomach to the next, and thinking about the olden days. Sal was proud to be a sheep, a member of the great and ancient family Ovis. She worried sometimes that the younger generation, even the four other Rare Breeds with whom she shared her paddock, no longer cared about their glorious heritage.

That had been her thought as she'd stood up to sing verse 167 of her favourite poem, 'Songs of the Fleece'. Then, quite suddenly, the lights went out. Of course, fields don't have lights as such, but that's what it seemed like. Sal felt a sudden sharp bang on the head and her legs buckled under her. Next, she saw flashing lights and bursting stars. Now, as she opened her eyes, she saw a little shadow. Had there been a different shadow, a bigger, blacker shadow, before the bang on the head? She wasn't sure.

The small shadow was caused by Wills. Wills was short and skinny, so he didn't block out much sunlight.

'Thank Aries you're alive!' he said, then turned to call the others. 'Over here, you guys. Sal's been hit.'

Wills' voice sounded faint in Sal's ears.

'Quickly!' he urged.

The others, who had been ambling across the field,

increased their speed to a gallop. They stood around Sal, wondering what to do. Jaycey noticed a tiny cut on Sal's head.

'Ohmygrass!' she exclaimed. 'She's bleeding.' She wobbled on her dainty hooves and fainted.

'Fat lot of help she is,' grunted Oxo.

Wills turned towards the farmhouse where their owner, Ida White, lived with Tod, her grandson. 'I'll fetch help,' he said.

But Sal called him back.

'No,' she groaned. 'Just dab me with a dock leaf.' She tried again to sit up. 'What happened?'

'Something fell out of the sky,' said Wills, 'and bounced off the top of your head.'

'I'm glad it didn't fall on *me*,' said Jaycey, recovering from her faint. 'Blood is soooo unattractive.'

Oxo and Links began looking around, though they didn't have a clue what for.

'Was it this?' asked Links. His searching nose had bumped into a small, silvery object with stud-like buttons and a square of blue plastic. There were words printed above the square: RAMROM.COM. Most sheep cannot read but Wills could because he had been brought up in the farmhouse kitchen.

'Ramrom dot com,' he read aloud.

'Dot what?' said Oxo. But he wasn't really interested. He was peering at the small golden symbol above the printed words: a picture of a ram's head. Sal peered at it too.

'It's a mobile phone,' said Wills, amazed.

'It's a ram!' exclaimed Sal.

'It's a ram *on* a mobile phone,' said Wills, correctly.

But Sal wasn't listening.

'A ram with golden horns . . .' she murmured. 'A ram with down-turned golden horns . . .' She turned to Wills. 'It fell from the sky, you said?'

Wills nodded. 'Yes.'

'And did you see a shadow?' she asked. 'Before it fell?'

Wills nodded again.

'Yeah, I saw it too, innit,' exclaimed Links. They had all noticed the loss of sunlight and the enormous dark shadow on the grass.

Sal looked at them gravely.

'Surely you see what this means?' she said.

Clearly they didn't. Sal struggled to her feet.

'You can't *all* have forgotten the ancient prophecy,' she cried.

They had.

Ignoring their blank looks and the pain in her head, Sal began to quote from the Songs of the Fleece.

'Whilst the great Lord Aries lies
In his field above the skies
With the Baaton lying near,
There's nought to fear.'

She paused, then started again, loudly, making Jaycey jump.

'But one day, Lambad the Bad,
Who is evil, maybe mad,
Will try to steal the Baaton
From our king!'

'Ohmygrass!' Jaycey's mother had often warned her about Lambad, the evil ram who eats lambs for breakfast.

'Yes,' said Sal. She fixed them with her yellow-eyed

5

gaze. 'I don't have to remind you about the Baaton, do I?' They shook their heads but she did anyway. 'It has a deeply magic power,' she explained solemnly. 'A power that can be used for good or for evil. Whoever owns it must decide. And only two sheep *can* own the Baaton: Aries the Good or Lambad the Bad.'

She drew a deep breath and continued reciting.

'For the Baaton they will fight,
For many a day and night,
Till to the prize they can no longer cling.'

She stood silent for a moment, then took another breath and started again. To her surprise, she heard other voices joining in, mumbling at first but gradually growing louder.

'Then from a shadow dark and cold,
Will fall the Baaton, it is told.
And the special Rare Breeds few
Will know what they must do.'

The sheep glanced uneasily at one another. Did that mean them? They carried on.

'For without the Baaton's magic rays,
The Ram of Rams will die in days.
Only *they* can save his life,
And the world from pain and strife.
They must be Warriors, brave and true!
Sheeply Warriors through and through!'

The voices that had joined Sal's trailed away again. The sheep stared down at the small silver object lying in the grass. Links was the first to speak.

'So like . . .' he asked slowly, 'are you sayin' this tingy's the silver Baaton of the *real* Golden Horn Dude? Aries, the Sheep Daddy of them all?'

Sal looked at him directly.

'Yes.'

Links backed away a little. They all did, respectful and suddenly afraid. Even Wills began to wonder. It still looked like a mobile phone. But although he knew a bit about such things and the ways of humans, he knew much less about sheeply prophecy.

'Brothers and Sisters of the Fleece!' proclaimed Sal. 'We have been called. Even now, Lord Aries is wandering the earth, getting weaker by the hour. We must find him and return the Baaton! If we fail, the future of sheepdom will be . . . zilch!'

The word zilch was not in the Songs of the Fleece but this was a vital moment. They had to understand.

'If Lambad lays his hooves on this, he will use its power against all wearers of the fleece. Just for fun, he will torment us with the unscratchable itch and turn our pastures to dust. Then he will give any of us who refuse to obey him to the dogs!'

Jaycey whimpered.

'So . . .' continued Sal, raising her head, 'we must find Lord Aries. And until we do, we must defend the Baaton with our lives . . . We must be Warriors, brave and true!'

There was a brief silence. The sheep looked at one another, each thinking that it was cauliflower night tonight. The human boy, Tod, would be bringing a barrow load for them at any moment.

'Are we sheep or are we sheep!' demanded Sal.

The others blinked.

'Then I shall go alone!' she cried, and trotted towards the fence, her fat hindquarters wobbling slightly.

'Wait!' Oxo, Links and Jaycey scampered after her.

At the fence, they all turned to look back at Wills.

'Wills?'

'Of course I'm coming,' he said. 'But won't we need the Baaton?'

He picked it up in his teeth and ran to join them.

Oxo stood facing the fence, pawing the ground with one hoof. 'Right,' he said, 'let's ship these sheep out. Charge!'

He crashed into the fence, turned a somersault and landed on his back on the flattened wire.

'Just making it easy for you,' he called, styling it out.

'Yeah right,' said Links. He and the others followed, treading on Oxo's tummy as they squeezed through the gap he had made.

They trotted off into the golden evening bravely enough but within minutes they had slowed to a walk. There was no hedge on the far side of this new field and without one they didn't feel safe.

'I think,' announced Sal, 'we need a bonding circle.'

'A what?' asked Oxo, backing away.

'Brothers and Sisters of the Fleece!' Sal suddenly cried. 'Let us join heads! One for five and five for one!'

She lowered her head, then, when no one else moved, she twisted her neck round and glared up at Oxo until he lowered his head too. 'Jaycey, come here between us,' Sal ordered. Jaycey stood between Sal and Oxo and lowered her own head.

'Don't scratch my lovely horns with your bony old skull,' she said to Oxo.

Links went and stood on the other side of Sal and she felt his floppy curls against her face as he too lowered his head. Wills squeezed in between Links and Oxo. He had to stand on tiptoe but he completed the circle.

'Baa . . .' said Sal, and the wheel of sheep, the tops of their heads pressed firmly together, woolly bottoms outwards, began to turn.

'Baa,' Sal repeated as she shuffled. 'Baa . . . Baa . . .'

The others joined in. 'Baa . . .'

Ever faster their bonding circle span and ever more loudly their baas rose into the sky.

'Baa . . . Lord Aries . . . Baaa . . . Your Rare Breed Warriors are coming . . . Baaaaaaaaa . . .'

And that's how aliens got involved.

2
Unidentified Flying Objects

There was a lane at the far side of the field in which the sheep were bonding, and in the lane was a tractor, driven by Tony Catchpole.

Tony was a farmer, but only because his family had always been farmers in Eppingham. He would much rather have been an astronaut. There was nothing he didn't know about space travel or Unidentified Flying Objects. He knew they were there. He just hadn't seen one yet.

Today, as Tony bounced along on his tractor, something unusual caught his eye. Something above Ida White's fields. He stopped for a better look.

The setting sun was shining in his eyes but there was definitely a roundish golden blur, hanging in the air. He shaded his eyes and beneath the dazzle saw something spinning on the ground. He squinted.

Sheep? A circle of sheep! He could hear them too, now he'd switched off the engine.

'Baaaaaaa . . .'

Dark clouds suddenly masked the sun and a brilliant shaft of light seemed to strike from the hovering blur in the sky, down to the ground where the sheep were spinning. But the glare was intense and Tony had to close his eyes for a moment. When he blinked them open again, the field was empty. The sheep had disappeared.

He hardly dared breathe. He squinted into the sky and thought he could see the golden blur moving swiftly into the distance. A thrill of excitement swept away his shock. He knew he must share this fantastic news with the world. He tapped a number into his mobile phone and held it to his ear with a trembling hand. At last there was an answer.

'Organic TV. How may we help you?'

Tony tried to stay calm.

'My name's Tony Catchpole and I've just seen a flock of sheep beamed up into a UFO.'

The Rare Breed Warriors heard the tractor roaring

away as they staggered out of the brook into which they had tumbled. The bonding circle had spun out of control. Now they all felt a bit giddy as they climbed back up the muddy slope to the sunlit grass.

Wills had managed to hang on to the Baaton. He put it down so he could speak.

'May I ask a question?'

Sal sneezed then nodded.

'The thing is,' said Wills, 'I understand *why* we're going. But not *where*. Where are we taking the Baaton?'

'To Lord Aries, of course,' said Sal.

'But where is he?'

Sal coughed slightly to hide her embarrassment. She hadn't thought of that.

'Well . . .' she began. 'Well. Lord Aries, Ram of Rams, is a Soay. And Soays live in the North.' She began to feel more positive. 'Yes, we must go North, to the place of jagged mountains and bare rocks, of howling winds and snow from which the first sheep sprang. We must go where even the thickest fleece is no protection against the elements and the weakest perish.'

'I can hardly wait,' muttered Oxo.

'Are we going to walk all the way?' asked Jaycey. 'I've only just painted my hooves!'

'Of course we're not going to walk,' said Sal. 'We shall use all the resourcefulness and cunning for which we sheep are rightly famous.'

They stood in silence, trying to think of a time when any of them had been resourceful or cunning. Then Wills spoke again.

'Um . . . Could I suggest that at the moment, the most cunning thing we could do would be to get out of this field and turn right at the sunset?'

'Quite,' said Sal. Then she blinked at Wills. 'Why turn right exactly, dear?'

'Because left would be South.'

'Absolutely,' agreed Sal. She looked at the others. 'You see. How cunning is that?'

Links nodded. 'Cunning as sheeps.'

He and Wills both raised a front hoof and clacked them together.

'Way to go, man,' said Links.

The other sheep joined in, even Sal. It was her first high hooves ever.

Then the Warriors trotted off towards the lane, taking the Baaton with them.

In the distance, a golden hot-air balloon was picking up speed in the freshening evening breeze and drifting away from Eppingham.

Some time later, the balloon began to lose height, then skimmed across the treetops as the pilot brought it in to land. The basket hit the ground with a bump and two passengers, young men in their twenties, tumbled out. One of them, whose name was Neil, was wearing expensive jeans and a designer jacket, and was clutching his bent sunglasses. His taller, skinnier companion, Luke, was wearing torn jeans, a faded T-shirt and a scruffy parka. Neil staggered to his feet and strode off without a word. Luke wiped his palms on the sides of his jeans and smiled awkwardly at the pilot.

'Sorry again,' he said, looking embarrassed. 'Didn't mean to upset you.' He gave a little wave, then ran off after Neil.

The pilot scowled. 'Next time Boyd's Bank give you a day off,' he shouted, 'go to the beach or something.'

Neil ignored him. He flung open the door of his flashy yellow sports car and stood glaring across the top of it at Luke.

'So. Why exactly *did* you chuck your phone out of the balloon basket?' he demanded.

Luke shrugged. 'Cos you said to get rid of it.'

'I didn't mean like that,' snarled Neil.

'What does it matter?' asked Luke.

'What does it *matter*?' shouted Neil. Some people nearby turned to stare.

Neil glared at them too, then slid into the driver's seat. 'Get in,' he snapped at Luke.

Luke lowered himself carefully on to the plastic bag that covered the front passenger seat. 'OK,' he said, trying to get comfortable on the slippery plastic, 'so I shouldn't have lobbed it over the side just because you didn't like my photos.'

'It had nothing to do with the photos,' growled Neil.

Luke looked puzzled. 'What then? It was only when I showed you the photo I'd just taken of you and the pilot that you went ballistic and said to get rid of it. Then when I did, you tried to climb out of the balloon to catch it!'

Neil took a few deep breaths and tried to calm down. He unbent his sunglasses and put them on.

'Forget the photos, Luke. Why was that *stuff* still on your phone?'

'What stuff?'

'What stuff . . . what *stuff* . . .?'

Neil's knuckles were white on the steering wheel. 'The stuff, Luke, that you hacked from the bank's computer? The account details, the security codes, the passwords, the PIN numbers . . .'

It was funny, thought Luke, how the human voice managed to get out through clenched teeth. Then he felt the g-force as the car took off like a rocket. He held on tight but he was still baffled.

'What's it matter?' he said. 'I only did it because you said I couldn't. I told you it wasn't impossible. Difficult but not impossible.'

Neil's teeth seemed to be grinding now. Then, after driving a mile in less than fifty seconds, he slowed the car to a halt. This time when he spoke, he sounded suddenly remorseful.

'The thing is, Luke, I have a confession to make. I owe you an apology . . .'

Luke was too surprised to speak.

'When you'd done the business yesterday – downloading all that stuff, all the bank details and everything, on to your mobile like you said you could – and you gave me your phone to prove it . . . Well, before I gave it back, I did something rather bad. I transferred some of the details on to my own computer. It's all gone again now – I've wiped it. But if anyone looks at your phone, they'll still be able to link it to me and what I've done . . .'

'Why?' asked Luke. 'What *have* you done?'

Neil sighed deeply.

'I borrowed some money. I needed a bit for my poor old mum, see. She's ever so poor, Luke, and she's got bad feet and lots of other bad bits that can't be fixed without cash. And she needs to be living in a little bungalow, not on the thirty-seventh floor of a tower block like she is now, where she can't even take her cat out for a walk. If she *could* walk, that is, which she can't because of her feet. But if anyone finds out what I've done, I'll go to prison and my poor old mum'll be marooned in the sky with her bad bits till she dies. And I won't even be able to visit her and take her a bowl of nourishing soup every day like I do now . . .'

Luke sniffed, then wiped his nose and eyes on his parka sleeve. He hadn't realised Neil's mum was so poorly. He hadn't even realised he had one.

Nevertheless, Luke was in a difficult position. He had hacked into the bank records and now money had been stolen. It was a serious matter.

'Of course,' said Neil humbly, 'I only took it from the accounts of really, really rich people. And only little bits they won't even notice. And it's not really stolen, only borrowed. I shall pay it back a.s.a.p. Every last penny. But until I do, your phone mustn't fall into the wrong hands. For my poor old mum's sake.'

Luke was overcome. He wiped his nose on his sleeve again.

'It's not a problem,' he said. 'I can work out exactly where it fell from the height/speed ratio of the balloon.'

'You can?'

'Easy.' Luke frowned in concentration for a moment, working out the arithmetic. 'Just follow the signs to Eppingham,' he announced. 'It must have dropped in a field near there.'

Neil started the car but Luke put out a hand and stopped him.

'Call her first,' he said with another sniff.

'What?' said Neil warily.

'Call your poor old mum and tell her everything's going to be all right.'

'Oh,' said Neil. 'Oh, right. Yeah. Thanks.'

He took out his own phone, smiled shiftily, and got out of the car. Soon, he was back. The call had been very short.

'How is she?' asked a concerned Luke.

'Who?' said Neil, startled.

'Your poor old mum.'

'Oh, right. Um. Out.'

'Out? I thought she was marooned on the thirty-seventh floor?'

'Out of earshot. She's deaf as well as everything else. Probably in the bath. I'll try again later. Let's crack on, yeah? Eppingham, you say?' The car leapt forward and roared away.

A little while later it had to screech to a halt to let a line of five sheep pass by in the opposite direction. One of them was making a funny noise. Luke leaned out to watch them go. Another one had a surprisingly silvery mouth.

'Did you see that?' Luke asked Neil. 'A sheep with fillings.'

3
The Aliens

Links would have been offended to know that someone thought he was making a funny noise when actually he was singing his latest rap. As the yellow car sped off, the rest of the Rare Breed Warriors joined in with him as he sang.

'We's the Eppingham Posse
And for your information
We's on a mission
To save the sheeply nation.
The Golden Horn Dude
Is deep in the doody
But Lambad's gonna split
Cos we's real moody.
The Warrior Sheeps
Is all fleeced up 'n' ready,

We's brave and we's true

And we's real rock steady . . .'

Sal had never rapped before but she felt as uplifted as the rest of the 'posse' by their 'marching anthem'.

'Way to go!' she cried, shaking a hoof approvingly at the nodding Lincoln. 'Totally fleeced up, man!'

They had turned right at the sunset as Sal recalled suggesting, and they were going so fast she was sure they would reach the North in no time. But then a strong seductive whiff of cauliflower came to them on the evening breeze.

Oxo was first to break ranks. He never forgot that a sheep's basic purpose in life is to eat. Quest or no quest.

'Comfort stop!' he shouted and plunged off the path, through a hedge and into paradise.

Cauliflowers stretched for miles, their white faces glowing in the dusk.

'Only one stomach full,' insisted Sal.

But her voice was lost beneath the general chomping. So was the rattle of a passing mountain bike on the other side of the hedge. Tod, the boy from

Eppingham Farm, was on his way back from football practice. It was almost dark when he got home. He dumped his football kit in the washing machine, then, as there was no sign of life in the farmhouse kitchen, called upstairs.

'I'm home, Gran.'

Ida White was actually Tod's great-grandmother and, as he was an orphan and only ten years old, also his guardian. Tod went upstairs and found her curled up on her bed. She opened her eyes.

'Hello, dear,' she said. 'Off to school?'

'No, Gran, I've just got home.'

Ida blinked. 'Really? I must have nodded off. That's what I get for sitting up with a sick hen all night.' She smiled hopefully. 'Does this mean I get lunch and supper all in one sandwich?'

Tod grinned. 'If you like. Shall I put the TV on?'

'No, dear, I can do it.'

Tod hurried back down to the kitchen to make Ida a mega sandwich. He loved his gran dearly and worried that she didn't look after herself properly. He looked around for the five pieces of fruit or vegetable the government said she should have every day. Lettuce, a slice of beetroot. So far so good but there was no more salad stuff. Some mashed banana, she liked that. Strawberry jam? Well, it was home-made with real fruit. He couldn't find anything else so he sprinkled a few cooked peas on to the jam and slapped on the lid of bread.

When he returned to her bedroom with the supper tray, Gran was sitting up, tutting at the TV screen, which was still blank. That was because she was waving her hairbrush at it, instead of the remote control.

'Specs, Gran?' suggested Tod.

She giggled as he found them for her and she put them on. Her tiny eyes twinkled behind the thick lenses. Gran was a thousand times older than anyone else Tod knew but also a thousand times more fun.

'The peas are nice and cold,' she remarked approvingly as they tucked in. 'Go very well with the banana.' Then suddenly, 'Oh, look. There's Tony Catchpole! What's he doing on the television?'

They had tuned in to the end of Organic TV's news bulletin. There indeed was a very nervous Tony Catchpole being interviewed by Nisha Patel, Organic TV's popular young female reporter.

'She's pretty,' said Gran. 'But I wouldn't wear a cream cotton suit in a farmyard. And look at Tony. He hasn't even washed his face. What that young man needs is a nice sensible girlfriend.'

It was Gran's habit to give a running commentary of the obvious whenever she watched television. Tod didn't usually stop her but this could be interesting.

'Sshh, Gran, let's hear what she's saying.' He upped the volume with the real remote.

'I'm Nisha Patel,' Nisha said into her microphone, 'and I'm standing here in the yard of farmer Tony Catchpole. Not far from where he had the most bizarre and exciting experience.'

She thrust the microphone under Tony's nose.

'Tony, tell us exactly what happened.'

Tony stared solemnly into the camera.

'Well, they wasn't acting like sheep normally do,' he said. 'They was in a tight circle on the ground and they was spinning faster and faster. Then –'

He flung his arm out to demonstrate what he'd seen and knocked the microphone out of Nisha's hand. It splashed into a puddle at her feet, sending a shower of brown sludge cascading over her neat cream skirt.

'Didn't I tell you?' chuckled Gran. 'Accident waiting to happen that suit was.'

'Beg pardon, Miss Patel . . .' Red faced and flustered, Tony bent to retrieve the microphone and handed it back. Nisha took it, glanced only briefly at the brown stuff now dripping down her arm, and continued with the interview.

'And what did you see then?' she asked, ignoring the ooze. And the smell.

'They just went around and around,' Tony said. 'Then they disappeared!' He leaned earnestly towards the camera. 'I didn't get a good look at the spacecraft. My eyes was dazzled, see. But there was this golden glow in the sky and then a beam of brilliant light shot down to the ground. It must have sucked the poor creatures up.'

Nisha didn't believe in UFOs but she did believe in treating people with respect. She was never rude to those she interviewed.

'And, uh, could you see how many sheep were actually beamed up into this UFO, Tony?'

Tony nodded. 'I wouldn't swear to it, mind, but I'm pretty certain there was five of them.'

'Five?' Gran looked at Tod and Tod looked at Gran. Then he turned the TV off.

'I'll, uh, just go and say goodnight to Wills and the others,' he said. 'It's cauliflower night tonight, anyway.'

Gran was creaking out of bed as fast as her old bones would allow.

'It's silly to be worried,' said Tod as they went downstairs and found their boots.

'Of course it is,' said Gran. 'So stop it at once.'

Tod hurried to the paddock, forgetting a torch as well as the cauliflowers. He called into the darkness as he walked.

'Wills . . . Jaycey . . . Sal . . . Oxo . . . Links . . .?'

'Oh my goodness. Oh my goodness . . .' Gran clutched Tod's arm. 'Look . . .' She was pointing at a gaping hole in the fence. 'What could have done that?'

Tod didn't know. He clambered through and paced every inch of grass in the paddock.

'They're not here, Gran . . .' he said when he returned.

'Well where are they then?' Gran's voice cracked and tears rolled down her cheeks. 'You don't think

Tony's right do you, Tod? Tell me they haven't been abducted by aliens.'

Tod patted her arm as they walked back to the farmhouse.

'Don't be silly, Gran,' he said to comfort her. 'What would aliens want with our sheep?'

But as he turned to close the farmhouse door, he saw two pinpricks of light dancing at the far end of the paddock that he'd just searched. Tod and Gran watched as the lights bobbed slowly towards them.

'Maybe we should call the police,' Tod whispered as the lights turned and bobbed back the way they'd come.

Gran shook her head.

'What can the police do against aliens?' she asked. 'No, we'll deal with this ourselves.'

She grabbed the broom that was propped in the corner and thrust it at Tod.

'Here, you have this. I'll take the mop.'

They hurried softly back towards the paddock and clambered through the hole in the fence. The lights were still moving slowly away from them. Tod and Gran followed silently, mop and broom at the ready.

As they got nearer, they saw that the lights were beaming from the foreheads of two dark figures.

'One-eyed monsters?' whispered Gran. 'Careful, Tod!' She occasionally remembered that as Tod's guardian she was not supposed to encourage him in dangerous activities.

The figures became clearer. They were bodies, human bodies, bent forward, peering at the grass as they moved across the field.

'Don't look like aliens to me,' whispered Tod. And he suddenly charged forward and rammed his broom handle into the back of the figure in front of him.

'That's my boy!' yelled Gran and she did the same. Her mop handle whumped into the back of the second figure, sending him sprawling face forward on to the grass next to his companion.

'What have you done with our sheep?' shouted Tod at his prisoner.

'Tell us where they are,' said Gran, prodding her captive in the back. 'Speak in alien if you like but tell us!'

4
Gran's Life Savings

Luke slowly turned his head to one side. Neil, flat on his face beside him, was pleading for his life.

'Don't shoot . . .' he begged into the grass. 'I can explain everything.'

Luke twisted around a bit further and saw that it wasn't an armed policeman pinning Neil to the ground but a very old lady in a nightdress and Wellington boots. She prodded Neil's back with her floor mop.

'They're Rare Breeds,' she said fiercely. 'Where have you taken them?'

Luke turned over and sat up, and Tod saw clearly now that he'd caught, not a one-eyed monster, but a scruffy young man with a head torch strapped to his forehead. The narrow beam of light from the torch bobbed up and down as the man moved his head.

'It's much worse than aliens, Gran,' Tod said.

'We'd better call the police, like I said.'

'Nooo!' The man under Gran's mop groaned into the grass but still didn't lift his head.

'We haven't taken your sheep. Honest,' said Luke. 'We're looking for my mobile phone. So that Neil's poor old mum can get her feet done.'

'What?' Tod wondered if they might be aliens after all.

The man under Gran's mop slowly raised his face from the grass, turned and sat up. His head torch had slipped down over one eye like a pirate's patch and he had a dob of sheep's poo on the end of his nose.

'It's a RAMROM,' Neil said, shifting the head torch. 'Silver colour. Where is it?'

Gran didn't like the way he spoke.

'Never mind your RAMROM,' she said, jabbing Neil's chest with her mop handle. 'What about my rams? Two of them. And two ewes and a lamb.'

'We've told you we haven't seen your mangy sheep,' snapped Neil, scrambling to his feet. He was bold and aggressive now he knew he was only facing an old lady and a boy. 'Just give us back the phone and we'll go.'

The old lady prodded him again with her mop handle.

'You'll go all right,' she said. 'This minute.' And she continued jabbing hard, forcing Neil backwards across the field towards the hole in the fence.

Luke didn't need any persuasion. Out in the lane, the head torches shone on a bright yellow car parked against the hedge.

'Open it,' said Gran.

'What! You think I'd hide your smelly sheep in here?' asked Neil incredulously, unlocking the doors.

'He's got white upholstery,' said Luke. 'Even I have to sit on a plastic bag.'

Tod and Gran checked inside the car but found no sign of sheep. Then they had to step back quickly as Neil started the engine and roared away.

'Don't come back!' yelled Tod at the tail lights. 'Or we *will* call the police.'

In the cauliflower field, Wills was wishing he hadn't asked Sal what Soays actually look like. Small and brown would have been fine for him. But not for Sal.

'Ordinary Soays,' she was saying now, 'are very

tough, of course, living in the coldest places, but the important thing is their ancientness, the fact that they could be called the ancestors of us all, and are therefore mentioned in many verses of the Songs of the Fleece . . .'

Behind her back, Links and Oxo were pulling faces at Wills, trying to make him giggle.

'Are you listening to me, Wills?' said Sal. 'What good are your human tricks, reading and things like that, if you know nothing about the roots of our sheepliness?' She sighed. 'When we've completed our mission and got back to Eppingham, I shall have to take you in hoof. A few hours' tuition every day.'

Links and Oxo snorted with laughter and looked away quickly in case they got a lecture as well.

Sal went back to her supper but Wills wandered uneasily over to the hedge. If they didn't move on soon, he thought, someone in one of the passing cars would spot them and they would be taken back before their quest had properly begun. They couldn't risk that. Not if Lambad the Bad was already out there in the darkness, hunting down the Baaton. Wills shivered.

*

In the farmhouse kitchen, Gran had finally warmed up.

'I suppose we're back to UFOs,' she said with a sigh. 'And you can't frighten them with a broom handle.'

Tod put four teabags in her mug and while they were brewing he wrote a notice for the village shop window.

MISSING

(POSSIBLY ABDUCTED BY ALIENS)

IDA WHITE'S RARE BREED SHEEP:

- ONE SOUTHDOWN. FAT. CREAMY FLEECE
- ONE OXFORD. HUGE. WHITE WOOL. BROWN FACE AND LEGS
- ONE LINCOLN LONGWOOL. BIG. LONG, CURLY FLEECE
- ONE JACOB. DAINTY. WHITE WITH BLACK SPOTS. CUTE HORNS
- ONE WELSH BALWEN. SKINNY.

BROWN WITH WHITE FACE AND FEET AND SMALL HORNS.

SMALL REWARD (GRAN'S LIFE SAVINGS) FOR INFORMATION

LEADING TO SAFE RETURN.

CONTACT EPPINGHAM FARM.

He wasn't sure that he should have put in the bit about Life Savings without asking first but Gran was pleased and perked up again.

'That's a good idea,' she said. 'I'd better find out how much I've got and have it ready. Now where's my laptop?'

'You left it in the barn playing music to the hens,' Tod reminded her.

'Did I? Never mind. I'll phone customer services. What's my memorable word, can you remember?'

'Something to do with feet, I think,' said Tod.

'Ah yes,' said Gran. 'Socks. That's it.'

She found the number for Boyd's Bank and tapped it into the phone.

'Would you like your tea first?' Tod gave the teabags a stir.

Gran glanced at the mug. 'Not yet, dear. Give them another minute or two.'

Her call was answered, she repeated her memorable word and listened for a few minutes. Then Tod saw her tremble and she had to sit down.

'You must have the wrong account,' she said into the phone. 'Ida J. White. I haven't taken out any money since Christmas . . . I see – well no, I don't see, actually, but . . . Yes. Yes, I will. Thank you . . .'

'What's wrong, Gran?'

'It's my money, dear,' she said. 'Apparently I did have six hundred and eighty two pounds. Then yesterday, every last penny was transferred to another account.'

'Why's that so bad?'

'Because I haven't got another account,' said Gran. 'And now it seems I haven't got any money either.'

5
Aries Calling

G ran and Tod were too shocked to think of anything but the missing money. They didn't hear the yellow sports car return or see the bobbing lights as the men with head torches crawled along the lane beside the sheep's paddock, fingertip-searching for their lost mobile phone.

The little beams of light bounced up and down and for the second time that night they were mistaken for aliens' eyes. Tony Catchpole was driving his tractor home from the Friendly Ferret pub. Perched beside him was Organic TV's Nisha Patel, clutching a daffodil that Tony had plucked for her from the roadside.

They'd had a very pleasant dinner. Tony had apologised again and again for the sludge, then knocked his beer over, spilling some into Nisha's lap. He had gone redder than ever. Nisha had laughed and said it didn't matter. She was still smiling now. She'd never been taken out for the evening on a tractor before. Then suddenly it lurched and stopped.

'D'you see that?' asked Tony.

Nisha peered eagerly into the darkness and saw . . . darkness.

'Dancing lights,' breathed Tony. 'They've gone now.'

Tony was torn. He would have charged off after the lights but he could hardly ask Nisha to come with him. Not in her high-heeled shoes and not after the sludge and the beer. She was, he thought, as beautiful as any UFO.

'I didn't see anything,' said Nisha, 'and I ought to be getting back to London now.'

'Yes, of course, I'll drive you to the launch pad – I mean the railway station,' babbled Tony, and he drove on, putting thoughts of aliens with glowing eyes out of his mind.

A few seconds later, a yellow car shot across the road in front of him and disappeared into the night.

There was an icy atmosphere in the car. Neil was driving too fast and tapping numbers into his mobile phone at the same time.

'You shouldn't be doing that,' said Luke, hanging on to his seat. 'Not while you're driving. Who are you calling?'

'My poor old mum, of course.'

There was no reply and Neil angrily threw down his phone.

'Still in the bath?' enquired Luke.

'Bath? Oh yeah. Still in the bath,' said Neil tersely.

'She'll be so wrinkly by now,' observed Luke. He became thoughtful, then, after a few seconds, grabbed Neil's arm, causing a near miss with a signpost.

'Hey!' he cried. 'Are we stupid or what? Why don't we try ringing *my* phone? If anyone's found it, they'll answer.'

The car screeched to a halt.

'Yeah,' said Neil. 'And if it's that kid and the bossy old fossil with the mop, well, we know where they live, don't we . . .?'

There was an edge to his voice that Luke didn't like.

Neil snatched up his phone. 'Remind me of the number,' he said sharply.

*

Oxo had felt nothing like it since the day he'd tried to eat an electric fence. His teeth were vibrating.

The Warriors had finally chomped their fill of cauliflower and were heading across the field back to the road. Oxo was carrying the Baaton in his mouth. But after only a few steps, it had started making a noise and now his whole head was jangling.

'Don't swallow it!' cried Wills, rushing to Oxo's side. 'Spit it out!'

Spitting things out didn't come naturally to Oxo and for a few more seconds he stood there with his teeth rattling and his eyes rolling, unable to move. Finally, he coughed and spat and the Baaton landed stickily on the grass. Oxo backed away rapidly and so did all the others. The Baaton lay there, vibrating and making a loud noise, its little blue square suddenly bright.

To Wills, the noise sounded like the first few bars of Farmageddon, the recent hit by Chickenslayer. Ida liked Chickenslayer and played them loud in the farmhouse kitchen when she was doing the ironing. If, after all, Wills thought, they were listening to a ring tone on a mobile phone, he might be able to switch it to answer. He put out his small hoof but Sal shoved him aside.

'Aries is calling!' she cried. 'Don't interrupt.' Wills backed away reluctantly and joined the rest in staring at the vibrating, glowing, noisy Baaton.

Inside the yellow car, Neil peered at the display panel on his own phone. He thrust it in front of Luke.

'That's definitely your number, right?'

'Yes.'

'Well, it's ringing but there's nobody answering. Who else but the old fossil and the kid could have found it?' He began to chew his fingernails. 'You don't reckon they've already taken it to the police, do you?' He chewed harder. 'Or what if they've sussed what's on it and are planning to blackmail us two and . . .' He stopped in mid-sentence and corrected himself. 'Us two and my poor old mum.'

Luke didn't think anyone would be heartless enough to blackmail an old lady with bad feet.

'We've got to get back to London,' said Neil, switching his phone off. He slammed the car into gear and drove off. Fast.

*

At the edge of the field, the Baaton fell silent. Links, who had soon got over his fright, carried on nodding to the music even after it had stopped.

'Cool . . .' he said, his long curls flopping rhythmically against his eyes. 'The Golden Horn Dude got some bangin' jams, innit . . .'

'Not jams!' cried Sal, who didn't know what jams were. 'Lord Aries was begging us to hurry!'

She snaffled up the Baaton and charged into the night. And into a painfully thick hawthorn hedge. The other Warriors, except Wills, piled up behind her.

'Is this the North already?' asked Jaycey at the rear, through a mouthful of Links' hindquarters.

'Uh, no,' said Wills, still standing a little away. 'But there's something here that might help us.' The moon had come from behind a cloud and lit up the wording on the side of a large lorry parked in the field.

'Eppingham Veg,' he read aloud. 'Feeding London.' He did a quick calculation in his head. 'London's north of here,' he explained. 'Not nearly far enough north but this could save us a day's walking.'

He was trampled in the rush. The back of the lorry

44

was open and its ramp had been left down. The sheep scrambled up. Once inside, they began burrowing their way into a pile of cabbages until they were hidden from sight.

'Yummy . . . pudding time,' chomped Oxo.

Sal began humming verse 222 of the Songs of the Fleece. It didn't exactly blend with the rap Links was singing but neither minded. Jaycey checked her hoof paint and wondered if London sheep would think her pretty. Wills began to plan what they would do once they got to the big city.

Nisha Patel was already on her way back to London. She dozed in her train, daffodil in hand, smiling about the sludge and the beer and wondering if there really were such things as UFOs.

Luke's journey to the capital wasn't as comfortable as Nisha's. Neil was driving too fast as usual. Luke hung on to the edge of his seat, hoping that Neil's poor old mum had got out of her bath. If not, she would be like a prune by now.

*

And in the farmhouse kitchen, Gran had drunk her cup of strong tea and got over the shock of her missing money.

'It's no good trying to deal with this on the phone,' she declared. 'We must go to London and have it out face to face with Boyd's Bank.' She turned to Tod as if launching a battle campaign.

'Oil the trikes, dear. We leave at dawn.'

6
Dogs Must Be Carried

The Warriors hadn't slept much, despite Sal droning out another fifty verses of the Songs of the Fleece. Links ignored her and composed a rap about vegetables:

'Now we's in a lorry and we's got the power,

Cos, man, we is like, full of sweet cauliflower . . .'

Then at dawn, the ramp had been slammed shut and they'd been thrown from side to side as the lorry travelled fast for some time. They'd bumped painfully into the sides of the vehicle and each other, and cabbages had bounced off their bodies and heads.

Now the lorry had slowed down again, stopping and starting as it crawled along the road. Cracks of bright daylight were showing around the edges of the side shutters. Traffic noise surrounded them. Wills judged that they had reached London. Once the back of the lorry was opened again, they would be clearly visible because, thanks to Oxo, there weren't many cabbages left. They must be ready to run.

Wills' knowledge of London wasn't great, but he'd heard Tod and Ida talk about a thing called The Tube and another thing called The Eye. Apparently, The Eye went round in a circle and could see everything. And The Tube went underground and squeezed millions of humans through itself.

The most famous thing about The Tube was its Map, and Wills knew the Warriors needed a map to find their way north. Turning right at the sunset worked only once a day. He tried to explain to the others.

'When we get out,' he said, 'we're looking for a sign.'

'Aries will guide us,' said Sal confidently.

'Not if he's ruckin' with the Lambad dude,' pointed out Links. 'The Eppingham Posse gotta be streety on its own, innit.'

'What's the grazing like in London?' asked Oxo anxiously. 'Is there any?'

'Will the shops be open?' wondered Jaycey. 'Can we buy a handbag for the Baaton?'

'Don't be silly, dear,' said Sal. 'Sheep don't have any money.'

'No,' said Oxo, 'we baater.' He began to chortle. 'Get it? Baa-ter. Baa-ter.'

'The sign we're looking for,' said Wills firmly, 'is a big red circle with a blue line across it. That means The Tube. With its famous Map. Have we all got *that*?'

The lorry swung right and then stopped. The traffic noise had faded. The engine went quiet.

'I think we're here,' whispered Wills. He picked up the Baaton. 'Geck reggy.'

'If we had a handbag,' said Jaycey, with the slightest hint of a sulk, 'we wouldn't have to speak with our mouth full.'

Then there was a scraping of bolts and the ramp crashed down.

'Mump!' cried Wills.

And he jumped from the lorry and ran. The other Warriors followed, leaping over and past a shocked driver. A couple of lonely cabbages bounced out behind them.

The sheep were in a market. Gorgeous vegetables and fruit and flowers were piled high on every side.

49

'Breakfast?' suggested Oxo hopefully, but Links butted him hard to keep him moving.

'Run, man,' he ordered, 'or we's all Sunday lunch.'

But the humans who worked in the market didn't seem interested in them.

'Clear off, you scruffy woolbags!' they shouted.

Jaycey, who was used to being ahhed over, was really miffed.

'It's because I haven't got a handbag,' she said. 'Everyone else has got one, look.'

It was true enough. They were out in the street now and each member of the human flock marching past them was carrying a bag of some kind or other.

Suddenly, the traffic stopped. There was a high-pitched peeping noise and a green light, shaped like a walking man, flashed on a post. The human flock streamed across the road towards a sign with a red circle and a blue line.

'The Tube!' cried Wills, dropping the Baaton in his excitement. 'They're going down The Tube.' He grabbed the Baaton between his teeth again. 'Mome om!' The green man turned red while they were crossing and the waiting cars hooted impatiently.

Oxo wanted to go head to head with them but, once again, Links butted him onwards.

'Save it for the Lambad dude,' he advised.

The entrance to The Tube was like a great shed. The human flock was now being sucked through it and down into a distant cavern.

The Rare Breeds struggled to stop themselves being carried along too, Sal holding the Baaton while Wills searched for The Map. At last he found it, but it wasn't at all what he'd been expecting; just a vast tangle of different coloured lines, with no mention of the North. Then he read a name he recognised. A name he'd heard in the farmhouse kitchen.

'King's Cross!' he shouted.

'So'm I,' replied Oxo, as humans continually bumped into him.

'Go with the flow,' directed Wills. And the Warriors allowed themselves to be swept along. Unfortunately, they soon interrupted the flow as there was a line of barriers right across the shed and they didn't have tickets to get through them.

'Use the luggage gate,' shouted the impatient commuters piling up behind. So the sheep struggled to one side. The man at the luggage gate opened it and nodded them through.

'Ramming them in this morning,' he said to his colleague. '*Ramm*ing them in . . . Get it?'

The human flock marched on, sweeping the Warriors along with it again.

'Ohmygrass!' Jaycey's legs turned to jelly and she wobbled and almost fainted. For real this time. Ahead of them were rows of steps. Moving steps. Some were coming up, coughing humans out at the top, and some were going down, carrying humans away to . . . she couldn't see where. The Warriors stood trembling with fear.

'Isn't there another way, dear?' asked Sal.

Wills didn't know. He saw a small sign at the top of the moving staircases.

He read it aloud, then wished he hadn't.

DOGS MUST BE CARRIED ON THE ESCALATOR.

'Ohmygrass!' Jaycey's legs finally gave way under her.

The last thing a sheep wants to carry is a dog. But looking around, Wills saw no dogs at all. Nobody was carrying one.

'I think we can ignore the dogs,' he said. 'But we have to go down.'

'Onwards then,' said Oxo bravely, and he galloped towards the nearest downward-moving staircase.

'Charge . . .!'

His front hooves scrabbled frantically on the metal step as they were carried away, leaving his back legs at the top. And those back legs, when they did follow, came too fast and he turned a spectacular somersault before tumbling down the stairs. Humans standing below looked up, saw a bouncing sheep and ran, taking the last few steps three at a time. Oxo fetched up in a heap at the bottom. He grinned dazedly at the other Warriors, gathered anxiously at the top.

'Easy,' he called.

The others copied the humans instead, stepping cautiously on to the stairs and standing still for the downward journey.

'Well, if you want to do it the boring way,' said Oxo when they joined him. 'Where now?'

There were tunnels in all directions, leading away from the cavern they now found themselves in.

They could hear deep rumblings and feel gusts of hot air.

'Is that you, Sal?' enquired Oxo. 'Too many cabbages?'

But Sal knew it wasn't her digestion. The wind grew hotter, the rumblings louder. She dropped the Baaton.

'Lambad,' she breathed fearfully. 'Lambad the Bad must be here . . .'

'Actually,' said Wills, studying the sign above one of the tunnels, 'I think this is the Victoria Line. And that's what we want.'

He led the way into the tunnel. They trotted quickly through and emerged on to a narrow platform with a dark hole at either end. This, Wills thought, with a mixture of fear and excitement, must be The Tube itself. A loud voice boomed somewhere above them.

'Mind the gap!' it commanded. 'Mind the gap!'

Jaycey, who was now carrying the Baaton, jumped.

'Ohmymaaaa!' she gurgled.

'Spit it out!' said Wills hastily.

She did and all the others gathered protectively around it.

'You need some help?'

The voice was human, though it sounded strange to the sheep's ears, and the hand placed on Jaycey's neck was gentle.

'Steady, gal,' said the voice reassuringly. 'Say, how cute is this, Billie-Jo? Sheep with a mobile phone.'

Jaycey panicked and tried to mouth the Baaton up again but she was clumsy in her haste and it slid across the platform.

The female human called Billie-Jo stooped quickly and picked it up before it fell over the edge.

'You've got a problem with that, I think,' she said kindly to Jaycey. 'Give me the map, honey.'

Honey, the male human who had spoken first, was carrying a map in a clear plastic drawstring bag. Billie-Jo took the map from the plastic bag, dropped the Baaton in and pulled the drawstring to close it. Then she hung it around Jaycey's neck.

'There,' she said. 'That should make life a whole lot easier.'

A delighted Wills bleated his thanks, but Jaycey scowled and tossed her head.

'This is *so* not a handbag,' she muttered angrily. 'I *wanted* a handbag . . .'

'But, Jaycey,' explained Wills, 'handbags are so last year. I saw it in Ida's magazine. It's neck bags now.'

'It is?'

'Trust me. Especially see-through plastic. You're cutting edge.'

'I am?'

Another hot wind riffled her wool as she tried to admire her new accessory. More humans were coming on to the platform. Jaycey could tell by the looks they were giving her that they knew cutting edge when they saw it.

'Cool . . .' she said happily.

'Mind the gap!' boomed the mysterious voice of The Tube.

Then the rumbling began again and this time it became a deafening roar. Suddenly, what looked like a giant metal worm burst from the round hole at the far end of the platform and thundered towards them.

'You guys definitely want northbound?' asked Honey as the metal worm came to a rest and the doors in its side hissed open.

Wills nodded and led the Warriors on-board.

Billie-Jo and Honey stepped on after them.

'Awesome!' said Billie-Jo. 'Even our sheep back home in the States aren't this smart!'

7
Eye Full

While the Warriors hurtled beneath central London on The Tube, Tod and Gran were above ground, pedalling rather more slowly towards Boyd's Bank.

Gran went everywhere on her trike and though Tod rode his modern mountain bike to school, he was proud to be tricycling beside her now. The machine he was riding had belonged to his great grandad, Albert.

The trikes were ancient, with large, heavy wheels, flaking navy-blue paint and rusty chrome handlebars. Each had a bell on the handlebar and a lidded container between the back wheels. Flying from the back of each trike was a small faded pennant with the slogan WE LOVE EPPINGHAM RARE BREEDS.

Tod and Gran had left the farmhouse before dawn but when they arrived at Boyd's Bank the pavement outside was already heaving with people. The crowd wasn't happy and a nearby newspaper billboard explained why:

BOYD'S BANK HIT BY SCAM –
MILLIONS STOLEN

Gran and Tod stood by their trikes, watching the crowd and listening to the angry shouts.

'D'you think they've *all* lost their Life Savings?' asked Gran, offering Tod a cup of tea from the flask they'd brought.

'Looks like it,' said Tod. 'The manager's going to be very busy.'

They ate mashed-banana sandwiches, drank the hot tea and waited. Neither noticed the two young men lurking not far from them, nor the yellow sports car parked further along the street.

Luke was still wearing his parka and didn't know why they were here. Neil had swapped his designer jacket for a hooded top and knew very well. Everything had started to go horribly wrong. His 'poor old mum' wasn't answering his calls and he needed information from Boyd's Bank. It was risky though, because both he and Luke worked there, and although they were officially on holiday, he didn't want to be spotted. Hence the hoodie. He peered around furtively and suddenly saw Ida and Tod. He dug Luke hard in the ribs.

'Look!' he growled, his voice low and urgent. 'It's the kid from Eppingham Farm. The kid and the old fossil.'

He watched them keenly for a moment.

'I knew they were lying,' he said. 'All that rubbish about sheep was just to get rid of us. I bet they've got your phone.'

He started pushing his way through the crowd. In all the hubbub it would be easy to confront the old woman, grab the phone from her and disappear.

Unfortunately for Neil, Organic TV got there first. A cameraman stepped in front of him as if he wasn't there. Then a pretty reporter started talking into the microphone she was holding.

'And it's not only the super rich whose money has so mysteriously disappeared,' she said solemnly. 'The anxious people waiting here for answers come from all walks of life.' She smiled at Tod and Ida. 'Good morning,' she said. 'Would you care to tell the viewers why you're here?'

Ida recognised the nice young girl who'd been talking to Tony Catchpole last night. She wasn't wearing the cream cotton suit this morning.

'Well,' said Ida, 'The thing is, Tod only wrote the notice for the village shop last night and now we'll have to change it.'

Nisha Patel looked slightly confused.

'Er, what notice would that be?'

She saw the tears welling in the old lady's eyes.

'We're offering a reward, dear.' Ida sniffed and steadied herself. 'Our little flock of Rare Breed sheep disappeared yesterday. Some people think it was aliens that took them, like Tony said.' She took a breath. The tears were finding their way down her wrinkly cheeks now. 'But we're not sure . . . All we know is we love them and want them back, so we were offering a reward . . .' She gulped. 'Only we can't now, because there's not a penny left in our bank account.'

Tod put his arm around Gran's shoulder. Nisha wanted to do the same. Neil ducked away before he got caught on camera. He tugged Luke's sleeve and they hurried back to their car. When they reached it, he saw that Luke was blubbing.

'What's the matter with you?' he demanded.

Luke used his parka sleeve before managing to speak.

'It's so sad,' he said. 'Even worse than your poor old mum. I hope the toerags who stole that sheep lady's money get caught.'

He was surprised to find himself suddenly banged hard against the car door. Neil's fists were clutching Luke's collar. His face was close. Very close.

'Listen, geek-o-nerd. You *are* one of the toerags. Right? You are in this all the way up to your spotty neck. Understand?'

Luke found it difficult to reply. Partly because he didn't understand; partly because he couldn't breathe.

Neil relaxed his hold a fraction. Luke swallowed. 'But what about your poor old mum?'

'There is no poor old mum!'

'You haven't got a mum? Then who have you been trying to phone . . .?'

'The boss!'

'What boss?'

'The Very *Nasty* Boss!'

Luke struggled to get to grips with this new reality.

Then he saw something that made him think he'd gone mad.

'Neil,' he whispered hoarsely. 'Behind you . . .'

Neil spun round, and there they were, trotting past the end of the street. Five of them. Assorted colours and sizes. Sheep. One of them had a plastic bag hanging round its neck. And in the bag was a silver-coloured mobile phone.

Neil stared in amazement, then his own mobile began to ring.

'After them!' he shouted, slinging Luke in the direction of the disappearing sheep. 'Get that phone!'

He took his mobile from his pocket while Luke stumbled off through the crowd.

Neil felt a moment of fear before answering. Was it the police? A blackmailer? Even the old fossil perhaps, demanding money for Luke's phone, which she'd cunningly hidden on her mangy sheep? It was worse. It was the Very Nasty Boss.

Neil panicked. The Very Nasty Boss listened briefly to him babbling on about old ladies with ancient trikes and sheep with mobile phones, then told him to shut up and finish the job. Fast.

The Warriors hadn't intended to come above ground when they did. Even Wills had found The Tube a bit confusing and they'd got off too soon at a place called Green Park.

'Green as in lush, juicy, life-giving grass?' Oxo had asked as they rode up the moving staircase, and suddenly everyone had remembered they needed food.

'It would be wise,' Sal had announced, 'to eat while we can. Empty stomachs lead to empty heads.'

And so, when Luke spotted them, they were following Oxo's nose towards the Green Park itself.

'Hey, guys,' said Links. 'I think we're being followed.'

Nobody was listening.

'Smell's getting stronger,' said Oxo, quickening his step.

'Definitely bein' followed, man,' warned Links, glancing around again. 'Guy in a baggy coat. Now another dude in a hoodie.'

But Oxo had only one thought in mind. He gave a couple of red buses a warning look and galloped across the road.

'Charge! One for five and five for lunch!'

And there before him was his reward: a large sloping field, dotted with trees. Even Wills joined in the general noisy grass ripping as the flock got down to business. He remembered too late what Links had been saying.

'What was that about being followed?' he asked.

As he spoke, Jaycey disappeared under something fur-lined and manky.

Having thrown his parka, Luke didn't know what to do next. Dare he pick it up again with the sheep inside? Did sheep bite?

'Grab it!' shouted Neil from a safe distance. Luke hesitated and Neil ran forward to push him in the back, making him fall on to the writhing, bucking coat. Then Luke got an answer to his earlier query. Did sheep bite? They did. One of them was biting him now. Another was trampling his legs. A third butted him in the ribs with a head like, well, like a battering ram.

Luke howled and rolled off the bucking parka. He heard the lining rip as the sheep scrabbled from underneath. Then he heard Neil shouting as all five sheep ran off, the phone still hanging from the black-and-white one's neck.

'You great wuss!' screamed Neil. 'Don't let them get away!'

Luke wasn't used to running. It wasn't what he did. His butted ribs hurt and so did his bitten bottom. He could hear Neil gasping for breath behind him but Neil kept going as if his life depended on it. Maybe it did, thought Luke. It wasn't a nice thought. He wondered briefly about the Very Nasty Boss and ran even faster.

'Keep together! Keep together!' panted Wills.

There was nowhere to hide. They were out of the park now. They ran across a street and through another park. They passed a huge clock on a tower, then galloped on to a bridge and across a wide river. They clattered down some stone steps and raced along the side of the river. Ahead of them was a huge wheel. They were charging with heads down now, to get through the people who were milling about. So many legs, so many babies in buggies. And still the footsteps pounded behind them.

Some people in black sweatshirts held out their arms and tried to bar Oxo's way. He crashed through, scattering them left and right, raced up a slope, leapt through the open doorway of a slowly moving glass cage and clattered to a halt. There was nowhere else to go. The others piled in behind him. The doors closed and the glass cage continued to move, slowly, smoothly upwards. They were being taken into the sky.

Huddled in a trembling mass, the Warriors stared out, faces pressed to the curved glass, watching the ground moving slowly further away and the clouds getting slowly closer. Below, they could see the people in black sweatshirts. They'd picked themselves off the floor now and were standing in a group, staring up.

Wills' heart stopped pounding quite so hard and he stepped back a little from the glass. Above his head he saw a notice:

WELCOME TO THE LONDON EYE.

So this is it, he thought. Nothing to be scared of, after all.

Then he realised that he could hear too many sets of panting, heaving lungs. He counted one, two, three, four, five . . . six . . . seven! He turned slowly. Trapped in the glass bubble, the Warriors were not alone.

'Right,' said one of the men. '*Now* get the phone.'

8
Methane Madness

The startled Warriors reared round. The two humans who had chased them were standing there, inside the rising glass bubble. The one in the hoodie was grinning unpleasantly.

'No escape this time, woolbags,' he said.

The scruffy one with the ripped parka didn't look so happy.

'The phone, Luke, get the phone,' repeated the unpleasant one, jabbing him impatiently.

'It is *so* not a phone,' bleated Jaycey, tossing her head so that the plastic bag swung from side to side. 'It's the Baaton. The Baaa-ton . . .'

'The Baaa-ton,' intoned Sal. 'The Baaa-ton. The Baaa-ton . . .'

And the whole flock took up the chant, even Wills.

'Baaa-ton . . . Baaa-ton . . . Baaa-ton.'

The noise bounced around the glass bubble as the sheep backed away, forming a solid wall of fleece around Jaycey and their precious sign from the Ram of Rams.

'Baaaaa-ton! Baaaaa-ton!'

Luke glanced nervously at the clear curved sides of the pod. The weird rhythmic din from the sheep was getting louder and louder. Luke knew about sound waves – they could shatter glass. He really didn't fancy a long drop into the River Thames. Especially with the tide out.

'Shush . . .' he heard himself saying. 'Shush . . .'

'Shush?' Neil bawled at him incredulously. 'They can't shush, Luke. They're sheep!'

Frustration finally got the better of Neil's cowardice. He threw himself at the flock like a rugby player joining a scrum.

Jaycey bleated in terror and the other Warriors closed up even tighter, turning their heads inwards, forming a protective circle around her. Neil suddenly found himself face to face with four woolly rear ends. It was then that their stomachs went into overdrive. Fear and last night's cauliflower combined to lethal, methane-gassy effect. Oxo was the first to pass wind. He couldn't help it.

Nor could any of the others. Neil suddenly staggered backwards, hit in the face by a noisy blast of wind from the woolly bottoms. Then came the smell, filling the pod, driving Neil inside his hoodie and Luke deep beneath his parka.

'Don't strike a match,' gasped Luke.

Falling into the Thames would be bad enough; being blown halfway to Brighton was something else.

By the time they dared poke their noses out again, the pod was descending. Neil saw the crowd on the ground below, staring upwards. He saw the cluster of Eye staff in their black sweatshirts, talking on their radios. He saw two policemen arriving.

'We're gonna get nicked,' he wailed. 'For hijacking The Eye.'

He made a last angry lunge at the sheep. They were facing him again now, but they shuffled quickly together, still protecting the phone, teeth bared, unblinking, defiant. Almost human. No, thought, Neil, that's the methane turning your brain as soft as Luke's. He shook his head and drew back again.

'Just don't lose them,' he said to Luke. 'It'll be easy back in the open.'

'You said it would be easy in here,' pointed out Luke.

'Stick with the woolbags,' snapped Neil. 'I'll do the talking.'

The landing platform was right outside now. The pod doors slid aside.

'Out!' barked one of the Eye staff. 'And bring your animals with you.'

'They're nothing to do with us,' protested Neil.

But as he stalked out of the pod and down on to firm ground, the sheep, led by the little brown lamb, trotted at his heels like obedient pets.

'They're not mine!' he insisted.

The staff crowded round Neil and as they argued, the sheep, still led by Wills, slipped quietly away.

They took a sharp left turn on to the pier next to The Eye, then increased their speed to a trot. The river boat at the end of the pier had cast its moorings and was about to move off. The sheep galloped the last few metres, then leapt one by one on to the stern of the departing vessel.

71

Their arrival on-board caused a bit of a stir, though most of the passengers seemed quite happy to budge up and make room for them. And there was no way the skipper was going to turn back now. He had a strict timetable.

The boat glided away from The Eye and the Warriors relaxed. Without a word, they raised and clacked high hooves. They had foiled the baggy coat and the hoodie. The Baaton was safe. For the time being.

'Is this thing going to take us all the way to the North?' asked Sal hopefully.

Wills didn't think so. He had seen the boat from The Eye and realised it was their best chance of escape. He hadn't thought beyond that.

'Sshh . . .' he whispered. 'Listen.'

The skipper was talking into a microphone.

'Welcome on board Thames River Boat *London Pride*,' he was saying, 'heading downstream towards the Thames Barrier. Now if you look back to your left, you'll see the famous Houses of Parliament where . . .'

The Warriors settled down. They might as well enjoy the trip and get a bit of education too.

Meanwhile, Neil and Luke had finally persuaded the Eye staff and the police that the sheep really didn't belong to them. Neil made Luke pay for both their tickets, and half an hour later they were free to go. But the river boat had long since disappeared around the bend, taking the sheep and the phone with it.

The two men walked along beside the river in silence. Luke put his parka on and ripped the lining even further.

'I've had a thought,' said Neil abruptly.

Luke hoped it would involve fleeing the country but it didn't.

'Correct me if I'm wrong, supergeek, but a mobile gives out a signal all the time it's switched on, right?'

Luke nodded.

'And it's possible to locate that signal?'

'If you've got the right equipment.'

'Well of course you'd need the right equipment. But *if* you had the right equipment, how close could you get? To knowing where the phone is?'

Luke shrugged. 'Depends on the distance between aerials. Out in the sticks, it could be miles . . .'

'In a city, Luke! We're in a city!'

'Oh, right. Yeah. Um, a few metres?'

'Excellent! Come on.'

'Where?'

'Back to the car.' Neil was already running towards the bridge.

The car was where they'd left it near Boyd's Bank but the street was almost empty now. The anxious crowds had dispersed and the television crews had gone. Inside the firmly closed glass doors of Boyd's Bank was a large notice:

NO FURTHER STATEMENT UNTIL TOMORROW.

Neil spotted the old woman and her grandson trundling slowly away on their ancient tricycles and remembered his earlier suspicions. He ducked down behind a parked van, watching them go.

'They surely can't know where the woolbags are now . . .' he muttered. 'But what if they do? Maybe we should follow them . . .'

As he spoke his thoughts aloud, the van moved away and he fell in the gutter. Luke tried not to laugh but failed.

'Plan A, geek!' Neil shouted angrily. 'Forget the

old fossil. We stick to Plan A like I told you.'

Then he ran to the yellow sports car. Luke followed, still giggling.

Minutes later, after twisting and turning down ever narrower backstreets, the car pulled up. Neil got out, ripped off his hoodie and put his designer jacket back on.

'Right,' he said, throwing the hoodie on to the back seat. 'I'll be back in five.'

And he disappeared through the rubbish-strewn back entrance of a shabby small office block. He was gone a lot longer than five minutes, but when he returned, he was grinning.

'Sorted,' he said. 'It's cost us, but from this very moment, my mate's tracking your phone.'

Luke glanced up at the closed blinds of the building. 'Is this legal?'

'Is bank fraud legal? Anyway, it's your phone. D'you object?'

Luke shook his head glumly and Neil started the car. He was in high spirits now and dabbed at his phone whilst driving one-handed.

'I've told you before about that,' said Luke.

'It's really dangerous.'

Neil ignored him and left a message on voicemail.

'Hullo, Boss,' he said breezily. 'Forget all that stuff about old ladies on trikes. We're back in business. Should be done and dusted by teatime.'

He chucked the phone on Luke's lap and continued driving.

'So where are we going now?' asked Luke.

Neil grinned at him. 'Following the boat, of course. Down river.'

Up the creek, more likely, thought Luke.

After a while the phone rang, making Luke jump.

'Answer it then,' instructed Neil. 'And if it's my tracker mate, write down everything he says.'

Luke did as he was told. When the call had finished, he read out what he had written.

'Greenwich.'

'There you go,' said Neil. 'They're probably still on the boat. Easy.'

He whistled a bit of Chickenslayer as he drove.

Half an hour later, the phone rang again and Luke dutifully answered it. This time, he didn't write anything down and, when the call had finished, he didn't say anything either.

Neil glanced at him. 'Well?' he asked. 'Where are they now?'

'Your mate's not sure. The signal's not good. Heading north, he thinks.'

Neil swerved and screeched to a halt.

'What? He's saying they're off the boat already?'

Luke managed a nod. 'Apparently so. And moving fast. Very fast.' He paused. 'He thinks they might be on a plane.'

9
Flight Zero One

They were.

When the river boat had stopped at City Airport Pier, Wills had seen the advertisement for FlyMe Airlines.

GOING NORTH? it asked. WHY NOT TAKE THE PLANE?

It was a fair question.

'Quick!' Wills had suddenly announced. 'This is our stop.'

The others, surprised and rather disappointed at having their pleasant trip come to an end, hurried down the gangplank after him. Wills explained what a plane was, as far as he understood it.

'It's like a bird with an engine.'

'What's an engine?' asked Oxo.

'It's the thing that makes a tractor go.'

Oxo frowned. 'I thought that was Tony Catchpole.'

'Look,' said Wills, 'that's all I know. Shall we try it or not?'

Links was nodding. 'Five for one and one for five . . . Let's fly, man, fly and stay alive . . .'

They set off for the airport. As they got closer, the noise of aircraft low overhead pressed down on them like thunder.

'Ohmygrass, ohmygrass . . .' whimpered Jaycey, worried that she would go deaf and no longer be able to hear the nice things people said about her.

Wills was worried too until he saw some planes on the ground in a long field. The closest one was much smaller than the rest and had its door open. Unfortunately, the strongest fence the sheep had ever seen was in the way.

Oxo was already pawing the road.

'Charge!' he cried, and hurled himself at the nearest section of ram-proof steel. He was the only one surprised when he bounced off it.

'Knew it all along,' he blustered. 'It's the digging-under variety.'

Sheep actually are quite good at digging, though

they rarely work as a team. They usually writhe under fences on their own so that they can get lost on mountains or fall over cliffs and then complain about it. But the Rare Breed Warriors were now very much a team and took turns to scrabble away energetically until they'd created a burrow a badger would have been proud of.

'Way to go, Warriors,' panted Sal through the dirt in her nostrils.

Once through and up the other side, they shook themselves relatively clean and trotted towards the little plane. The word EATWELL was printed on its side. There was a large trolley beside it and boxes were being carried on-board by a young woman in a smart uniform. She turned and stared at the sheep and then called to the pilot sitting in the cockpit.

'I thought we were taking frozen lamb,' she said. 'What d'you think about this lot, Nikki?'

Nikki, the pilot, peered down at the sheep.

'I suppose fresh is better,' she said. 'Get them loaded, Sarah.'

Sarah ushered the Warriors up the little flight of steps into the plane. Then she climbed in after them, pulled the steps in behind her and closed the door.

'Right,' she said. 'Welcome aboard Flight Zero One to the Eatwell Hotel, Yorkshire. Your pilot today is Nikki and my name's Sarah. I'll be looking after you during your journey. Shall I help you with your seatbelts now?'

Once she'd done so, the plane taxied swiftly on to the runway, then took off.

'Whoa . . .!' exclaimed Links. 'Did I leave one of my stomachs back there . . .?'

But he was soon nodding and singing.

'We's the Eppingham Posse
On a mission for the Nation,
We's high in the sky
An' for your information,
The Baaton's goin' home
To the Golden Horn Dude,
Got a message for the Lambad
But you'll think it's kinda rude –'

'Drink, sir?' Sarah was holding a plastic bucket full of iced water in front of Links. He lapped it gratefully.

Then she gave each of the sheep a lettuce from one of the cargo boxes. And an apple.

'Yum. We should have done this flying thing before,' said Oxo enthusiastically.

In the yellow sports car, Luke was enjoying himself rather less. Neil's phone tracker mate had rung again to confirm that things would most certainly not be done and dusted by tea time. The missing mobile was now cruising somewhere above the Midlands.

Neil glanced at Luke. 'Did you pack your toothbrush?' he asked.

'No.'

'Tough.'

'Neil,' said Luke, 'a car cannot chase an aeroplane.'

'Wanna bet?'

The g-force kicked in again and they streaked away, not so much like a rocket this time, but like a sheep-seeking missile.

On the other side of London, things had just got worse for Tod and Ida.

The pedals on Ida's trike had suddenly spun

madly and she'd coasted to a full stop. Her chain had snapped.

'Never mind, Gran,' said Tod. 'I can give you a tow.'

Gran was tired but she smiled back. 'A whole foot would be better.'

Tod grinned at her brave joke and started tying some cord on to Gran's handlebars.

As he tied the first knot, a car passed by, then reversed and came silently to a halt beside them. It was a very large, swish car. A smartly dressed lady got out and smiled kindly.

'Can I help?' she asked.

'I doubt it, thanks,' said Tod. 'The chain's gone.'

'Oh dear,' said the lady. She frowned at them both then said, 'Didn't I see you on television at Boyd's Bank earlier? Weren't you being interviewed?'

'Yes,' said Tod. 'Gran told Organic TV about our sheep.'

'Yes, of course! The sheep. How terribly upsetting.' The lady looked with concern at Ida, who had sat down wearily at the roadside. 'Have you got far to go?'

'Eppingham,' said Tod.

'But that's miles away.'

'We'll be all right,' said Tod, tying the cord to the back of his trike. 'Gran's no weight. I'll pull her along.'

The lady hesitated a moment.

'Look, why don't you come home with me for a rest? You can even stay the night, if you like. I've got plenty of room. Don't worry about your trikes,' she added. 'I'll call someone to collect them right now.'

Tod didn't know what to say but Gran drew a deep breath and stood up again.

'That's very kind of you indeed,' she said, taking charge. 'And we don't have to be back to feed the sheep. Not now they've been abducted by aliens. We might as well rest for a bit and work out what to do next.'

'Excellent,' said the lady. She nodded firmly. 'My name's Caroline, by the way. Lady Caroline Babcott.' She made a swift phone call and within minutes a van arrived and two men carefully loaded the trikes on to it. Then Lady Babcott held the car door open and Tod and Gran stepped inside.

'It's as comfy as your bed,' Tod whispered to Gran.

'And almost as big,' Gran whispered back, as

84

Lady Babcott started the quiet engine and the car moved smoothly away.

The sheep were still enjoying the high life, taking turns to peer out of the aircraft's small windows at the carpet of countryside unrolling beneath them. Then they heard Nikki's voice over the loudspeaker. She was talking to someone at the Eatwell Hotel, Flight Zero One's destination.

'ETA three minutes,' she said. 'No customers today, just catering supplies.'

Wills stiffened slightly. What were catering supplies? Was that just another name for lettuce? He hoped so.

The plane lurched slightly as the wheels hit the ground. It bounced along for a few moments, then swung round and taxied back towards the large grey-and-white building the sheep had glimpsed as the plane had circled down.

'Welcome to the Eatwell Hotel.' Sarah was beaming at them. 'Thank you for flying with us this morning. Please remain in your seats until the butcher arrives – I mean until the aircraft has stopped moving.'

Sarah put down the steps and Nikki came through

from the cockpit and climbed out first.

'See you at dinner time,' she called as she hurried away.

Sarah smiled and nodded politely at each of the sheep in turn as they too left the aircraft. 'Follow me,' she said and headed towards the hotel.

'Well, how pleasant,' said Sal, as they trotted along behind. 'And now we're in Yorkshire. Remind me where that is exactly, Wills.'

'Quite a long way in the right direction,' said Wills, not paying full attention.

A door at the back of the hotel was open and inside it he could see men and women in white jackets and hats. The word catering came back into his head. Catering happened in kitchens. He heard the unmistakable sound of knives being sharpened. Catering plus knives, plus butchers, plus sheep could mean only one thing.

'Chops!' he cried.

The other Rare Breeds stopped dead. Chops was the only word they feared more than Dog.

A man in a white jacket and tall hat came out of the kitchen, knife in hand.

'Run!' yelled Oxo.

He charged across the hotel flowerbeds towards the nearest neatly trimmed hedge and ploughed straight through it, leaving a ram-shaped hole for the others.

'Hey, where d'you think you're going?' yelled the chef.

He ran a few steps after them then stopped. He was far too important to go chasing animals.

'Roast lamb's off,' he called to one of his assistants. 'We're doing nut cutlets instead.'

The Warriors kept running until they were well away from the hotel and then slowed to a walk.

'Sorry,' said Wills, 'I should have remembered what catering was a bit sooner.'

'Relax, man,' said Links. 'We's not chops, innit. We's still fresh on the hoof . . .'

'Ohmygrass, stop talking about it,' bleated Jaycey as she hurried on.

'Yeah,' said Oxo with a grin. 'Chop chop.'

The path they found themselves on led down into a valley, and along the bottom of the valley ran two metal lines. Wills stopped for a moment.

'That's a railway,' he pointed out. 'Maybe we could get a train from here.'

But before he could explain about railways and trains, he heard a rattling noise behind him and a shout which became a frightened wail. They all turned and saw a boy on a mountain bike careering down the path towards them. For a moment, they thought it was Tod, but it wasn't.

'No brakes!' cried the boy, half in warning, half in terror.

The sheep scattered as the bike sped on down and hit the railway fence, catapulting its rider on to the track beyond. He landed heavily and lay still.

The Warriors raced down after him.

'Ohmygrass . . .' Jaycey stared through the wire at the crumpled human. 'Ohmygrass . . .'

Oxo finished the job that the bike had started on the fence, muscling his way between the broken, rusty strands. The other sheep joined him. They each gave the motionless boy a comforting lick but he didn't stir.

Then Wills' sensitive hooves began to tingle ever so slightly. The metal rail on which he was standing had started to vibrate. He tried to stay calm.

'Uh, guys, I think we should try to move him. There's a train coming.'

'Ohmygrass, ohmygrass,' squealed Jaycey. 'Train train train!'

She didn't really know what a train was but there was no doubting the urgency in Wills' voice. They all tried hard to roll the boy to safety. But no matter how they struggled, pushing their noses underneath him and lifting on the count of three, they couldn't get him over the raised metal line.

The Warriors could all feel the vibration now. Wills looked desperately around. On the other side of the track was a small, sloping meadow. And halfway up the steep slope was a wagon piled with hay bales.

'Jaycey, keep licking him,' said Wills. 'Everyone else, come with me!'

There was only a straggly hedge on the other side of the track. They pushed through easily and galloped up to the wagon. Wills stood behind it and lowered his head. 'Butt!' he cried. 'Butt like the Ram of Rams himself!'

The four Warriors lowered their heads and charged the wagon, crashing into it head on. They tried again and again. Finally, as a distant noise became a clearly approaching train, the wheels of the wagon began to turn.

'Keep pushing!' gasped Wills.

The wagon creaked and moved a little. It moved a little more, then gathered pace until the sheep could no longer keep up with it. Then it trundled down the slope like a runaway juggernaut. They watched, breathless, as it smashed into the straggly hedge and its load of hay bales tumbled across the railway line, bursting as they bounced.

The train driver would never have seen the small boy. But he couldn't fail to see the mountain of hay. He applied the brakes full on. The train screeched and crackled, then came to a halt inside the soft, yellow mountain.

On the hillside above, the four Warriors let out a bleating cheer. Jaycey came bounding up to join them.

'The boy's awake,' she called. 'He smiled at me.'

It was a moment for high hooves all round.

In the security control room of the Eatwell Hotel, the man on duty was staring goggle-eyed at his CCTV screen. One of the hotel's cameras faced the railway. The man stumbled from the room and grabbed the first person he met.

'Those sheep we're not having for dinner. They just stopped a train. On purpose!'

10
Luke's Big Decision

There was rather good grazing on the sloping meadow and the sheep took the opportunity to have a quick snack.

While they munched, they watched dozens of humans get out of the stationary train and dozens more run down the path from the hotel. The emergency services arrived soon afterwards, even though, thanks to the Rare Breed Warriors, the emergency was over. The boy was on his feet now, surrounded by the excited humans, some of whom looked up at the meadow, saw the sheep and started climbing through the fence towards them.

Wills wasn't sure if this was a good thing or not. The word catering came back into his head. Then Chops.

'Shall we go?' he suggested.

'Right on, dear,' agreed Sal. 'Let's get questing. Uh, which way is the North again?'

'Away from the humans,' said Wills. But it was a guess.

The sheep disappeared rapidly over the hilltop, completely unaware that they were suddenly big news.

Almost the entire nation saw them on television that very night. There was the CCTV footage from the hotel. There were interviews with the rescued boy and the train driver. There was a panel of animal experts who earnestly agreed that a Quantum Leap in Ovine Evolution had taken place.

Organic TV's Nisha Patel, who'd been flown north especially to cover the story, frowned at the long words.

'You mean they're sheep like sheep have never been before?'

The experts nodded.

'Exactly.'

'Super strong.'

'Super intelligent.'

'Bionic, thinking, super sheep.'

In his sitting room at Hogweed Farm, Tony Catchpole couldn't help shouting at his television set.

'You're not asking *why!*' he yelled at the experts. 'You're not asking *how!*'

Because Tony knew very well. He recognised the sheep and to him it was obvious: they'd been modified by the aliens who'd abducted them.

Nisha Patel's face reappeared on the screen and Tony tried not to blush. He wondered if she still had his daffodil. He tried to concentrate. He desperately wanted to find those alienified sheep. Almost as much as he wanted to see Nisha again. He glanced at his watch and then rushed to catch the train.

Tod and Ida were also watching the news. It was like being in a cinema, Lady Babcott's TV set was so big. Her whole house was huge. She had given them lunch, then supper, and then arranged to have Gran's trike fixed for the next day. It seemed sensible to accept her kind offer and stay the night.

Lady Babcott was watching television with them. She noticed Tod grasp his grandmother's hand when they saw the CCTV pictures of the sheep.

'Are those yours?' she asked in astonishment.

Tod and Ida both nodded. Then Tod recovered and grinned.

'See, Gran,' he said. 'They haven't been abducted by aliens after all.'

'It doesn't look like it,' said Gran, peering through her specs. 'But what's that thing hanging round Jaycey's neck?'

Tod peered too and shrugged. 'No idea,' he said. 'And how have they got all the way to Yorkshire?'

It was Gran's turn to shrug. 'Maybe the aliens dropped them off there when they'd finished with them?'

Tod gave her a little nudge. 'You're getting as bad as Tony Catchpole, Gran.' Then his face became more serious. 'I think we should tell the police,' he said. 'They'll help us get them back.'

'Of course,' agreed Lady Babcott. She waved her hand and her butler carried the phone across to her.

'Here you are, my dear,' she said, offering it to Gran. Then she suddenly stopped and took it back again. 'Wait! I've got a better idea. The police will be so terribly busy with the bank fraud, they might not have time for your sheep. Why don't *we* get them back?'

'How?' asked Tod.

Lady Babcott smiled. 'I'll cancel all my meetings tomorrow and take you up to Yorkshire myself.'

Just about the only people who didn't see the news were Neil and Luke. All they knew was that the signal from the missing phone had been tracked to Yorkshire. So they were hammering up the motorway in the yellow sports car.

Luke was dozing when Neil's phone rang. Clearly, from Neil's response, the call was from the Very Nasty Boss. Even nastier than before. When the call had finished, Neil poked Luke in the ribs.

'Those woolbags,' he said. 'Apparently, they're not just sheep. They're bionic, thinking super sheep.'

'Oh,' said Luke. As if he didn't have enough to worry about already.

The moon had risen before the Bionic Thinking Super Sheep finally stopped to rest. They settled down beside a dry stone wall and chewed the cud for a bit. One by one their heads began to droop.

'We should take turns at keeping watch,' said Wills suddenly. 'To keep Jaycey and the Baaton safe.'

'Good call, man,' said Links, raising his head again. 'I'll go first.' And he shifted himself next to Jaycey.

'Oh,' she said, all of a flutter. 'Oh, I can't imagine why you want to sit close to me, Links – I'm *such* a mess, what with the travelling and rushing about. My fleece is in knots.'

Links made no comment. Either he was breathless with admiration or had gone to sleep again. A deep snore told Jaycey which.

Neil finally stopped driving when he and Luke arrived near the Eatwell Hotel. He couldn't stay awake any longer, and even he didn't claim to be able to drive when asleep. He parked in a lay-by and was still snoring at dawn. He didn't notice Luke slip quietly out of the car and plod off through the rain.

Luke had made a decision. He was going to give himself up. He didn't care if he went to prison. He didn't care what Neil said. He didn't even care about the Very Nasty Boss. He felt guilty and ashamed about the bank fraud, about the people whose money had been stolen; and most of all about the old lady who'd lost her sheep as well as her Life Savings.

There was a small police station in the local village. Luke braced himself, held his head high and strode right up to it.

11
The Sheepdog

Unfortunately, the police station was closed.

Luke sat on a bench in the now pouring rain and waited, but nobody came. The forces of law and order seemed to be having a lie in. Gradually, Luke began to change his mind. Perhaps giving himself up was a bad idea. If he could get his hands on the phone, he might be able to trace where Neil had diverted all the money. Probably, it had gone to an account owned by the Very Nasty Boss. Luke might be able to divert it back again. To its rightful owners. To the poor old sheep lady.

He returned to the car and slid back into his seat. He was soaking wet and the windows soon steamed up. A group of early-morning school children giggled as they passed, then banged on the roof.

'Give us a kiss!' they yelled, and ran off.

Neil woke with a start.

'What was that?' he snapped.

Luke shrugged. 'Just kids.'

Neil frowned at Luke's sodden parka.

'Where have you been?'

'Nowhere.'

'Well, go back again and find us some breakfast.'

Tod and Gran had already finished their breakfast, and very nice it was too. No cold peas but Ida could live without those for a day or two.

'Right, off we go,' said Lady Babcott, striding out of the dining room and heading up the grand staircase.

'Why are we going this way?' whispered Gran. 'She left the car in the garage.'

She found out when they stepped on to the flat roof of the house. In front of them was a helipad with a bright-blue helicopter sitting on it.

'Wicked!' Tod breathed.

'Ever been in one before?' asked Lady Babcott.

Tod and Gran shook their heads. Soon they were side by side in the back seat, with headsets on, and

Lady Babcott was in the front, turning switches, ready for take-off.

'All belted up?' she asked into her radio mike.

'Roger, Roger,' Gran shouted excitedly into hers.

Lady Babcott winced. 'You don't have to shout into the mikes, dears,' she said. 'Just speak normally.'

'It's brilliant!' replied Tod, but it was impossible to sound normal.

Gran grabbed his hand tightly as the helicopter rose into the air. 'Wheeeee . . .!' she cried.

Lady Babcott expertly banked the helicopter and the helipad seemed to twist and shrink beneath them.

'Wheeeee . . .! Tod replied, squeezing Gran's hand. 'This is even better than Eppingham Fair!'

'And we'll be able to see for miles,' said Gran, gazing eagerly ahead.

'Exactly,' agreed Lady Babcott. 'We'll find those sheep in no time.'

Far away in Yorkshire, the Warriors had woken early and were munching the moorland grass. It was short but tasty and, unlike Luke, they didn't mind the rain. Wills was anxious though, in case the humans from

101

the train and hotel were still looking for them. He was relieved when the clouds parted and a trace of silvery light told him what he needed to know.

'That's the sun rising in the East,' he called as he trotted away. 'So it's this way to the North.'

The others were soon scampering after him, but as the morning passed, the sun disappeared behind thick cloud again. The weather became colder and even wetter and eventually the sheep's spirits began to droop in the damp.

'Hey, Links. How about a rap?' asked Wills.

'It's comin', man . . .' murmured Links, already nodding his head. Then he shook his soggy curls and began to sing.

'The Eppingham Posse is up on the moors,
Cos we ain't ruled by no human laws.
We's goin' to the North
An' he can laugh or what,
Cos when we meet that Lambad,
We's gonna butt him in the butt . . .'

The others joined in and it was their singing that

Saffron first heard. Saffron was a sheepdog. She pricked up her ears and began to bark.

'Stop that,' snapped Jason Pitt, her owner. 'And don't go charging off or we'll miss the train.' He stalked bad-temperedly towards the station.

Jason was not a sentimental man. He had a lot of sheep and needed a good sheepdog. Saffron was not a good sheepdog. She was pretty, that was true. And she had a nice nature. But she was stubborn, and if she didn't feel like rounding up sheep, she would just lie down and refuse to budge. Jason was on his way to sell her.

The Warriors all heard the bark, somewhere below them. They stopped in mid-rap and huddled together.

'Ohymgrass . . . Dogdogdog . . .' bleated Jaycey.

'Sshhh . . .' said the others.

Wills led the way quickly uphill where the misty rain and cloud merged into an all-concealing fog. They were on the very top of the moors now and soon the fog became thicker still. The Warriors plodded on uncomfortably through shifting white walls of it. They could no longer hear the dog but Wills began to worry that they were going round in circles. There were no landmarks, not even walls or hedges. Just themselves, wandering in a chill, opaque wilderness.

Wills slowed to a halt. The others also stopped.

'What's up?' asked Oxo. Then he saw it too.

Sitting silently on the ground in front of them, its large ears laid back, its huge eyes unblinking and its even huger teeth bared, was the biggest sheep they had ever seen.

12
Lama Glama

'Is it the Lambad dude?' whispered Links.

'Just bring it on, if it is . . .' muttered Oxo, pawing the ground.

Somehow, Wills hadn't imagined Lambad chewing the cud. Or humming to himself. The biggest sheep they had ever seen continued to do both while it stared at them. Finally, it swallowed and spoke.

'Ovis Aries, I presume.'

'Don't get funny with me, mate,' said Oxo.

'We are of that species, yes,' said Sal quickly. 'Rare Breeds,' she added.

'Warriors, innit,' said Links.

The creature nodded, then stretched out its neck towards them for a better look. The Warriors gasped and stumbled backwards in shock. What kind of sheep had a neck as long as *that*?

'Lama Glama,' it said.

'Pardon?' said the Warriors.

'My species. Lama Glama. Llama for short. Unlike my neck.'

'You're a llama?' said Wills.

'I'll ask the questions,' the llama replied. 'It's what I do up here when not dreaming of my Andes.'

'Is she your girlfriend?' asked Jaycey.

'That's a question,' the llama said. 'Your only concern is answers. Tell me: My first is in path but not in way. My second is in eggs but not in hay. My third is in rain and also in right. And my fourth is in up but not in down. What am I?'

'That last line doesn't rhyme, man,' said Links. 'You need something that goes with right, innit?'

'Sshh.' Wills was thinking hard. 'Uh . . . P . . . The letter P is in path but not in way. E. The letter E is in eggs but not in hay. R. That's in rain and also in right. And, er . . . U. The letter U for up. P . . . E . . . R . . . U . . . Peru !'

Lama Glama nodded.

'It's a country,' whispered Wills to the others. 'Where llamas come from.'

'Here's another,' said Lama Glama. 'Mirror, mirror on the wall, whose is the finest fleece of all?'

'Ooh. Easy peasy,' said Jaycey, tossing her head. 'A Jacob's, of course.'

'A Jacob's is the wrong answer,' said Lama Glama and he spat, but only at the ground, and only from his first stomach.

'It is so *not* the wrong answer,' protested Jaycey.

Wills gave her a nudge. 'Shut up,' he murmured. This was not the moment for hurt pride. 'A llama's?' he ventured.

Lama Glama nodded. His long neck waved around a little, as if he were scanning the fog-shrouded hilltop.

'If two men are creeping up the slope towards you,' he asked, 'how many ways are there for you to escape?'

The sheep pondered for only a second then wheeled around in alarm. They could see nothing through the fog but now they could hear approaching footsteps, squeaking across the wet grass.

'The answer,' said Lama Glama, getting to his feet, 'is only one. Follow me.'

And he trotted away into the murk. The Warriors looked at each other, then followed.

Lama Glama led them on to a narrow downward track, steep and slippery and barely two hooves wide. Down and down they went in single file, struggling to keep up with his long, sure-footed stride. They could hear the men clearly now, tripping and slipping and cursing somewhere behind them.

The ground began to level out and suddenly they could see a building through the mist.

'Railway station,' announced Lama Glama. Then: 'The answer is twelve. What is the question?'

'How many legs on four sheep?' asked Jaycey, glancing around nervously.

Lama Glama shook his head.

Wills could hear a train coming. 'Departure time?'

Lama Glama nodded. 'Good question.'

The train rattled noisily towards the station, but as it arrived a dog began barking excitedly. Saffron had picked up the sheep's scent again. The Warriors could see her now. The dog and her man were running along a lane towards the station entrance. And looking back up the hill, the Warriors could also see the two men who'd tried to capture Jaycey in London. They were catching up fast.

'Go, go!' yelled Oxo and he charged on down the hill after Lama Glama. Sheep and Lama hurtled through the gateway on to the station platform and skidded to a halt. The Warriors closed protectively around Jaycey, then turned defiantly to face their pursuers.

The two men from London reached the gateway at exactly the same time as the dog and his man. All four tried to bundle through together and got stuck in a tangled mess of arms and legs.

'Out of my way, moron!' panted Neil.

'Out of *my* way, stupid!' snapped Jason.

Saffron barked even louder and squeezed her way through.

On the platform, the sheep turned desperately back to the train. Its doors hissed open and, as one, they leapt on-board.

'Guard's van is in the middle carriage,' Lama Glama informed them. 'The snacks trolley always starts from the rear.'

The dog was bounding along the platform now.

Lama Glama didn't move from his position in front of the open train door.

'What do I wish you, Ovis Aries?' he asked.

'Uh, have a nice day?' Jaycey was wrong again.

'May the Luck of the Llamas be with you,' Lama Glama replied. Then he added, 'And I spit in the eye of your enemies.'

'Cheers, mate, nice one,' said Oxo, and the train doors hissed shut just as the dog and all three men raced up to it. The dog leapt at the doors, barking frantically and Neil pushed past the llama, trying to reach the 'Door Open' button.

'Move!' he yelled angrily.

'Mwa . . .' grunted Lama Glama in the dangerous way that llamas have, and he produced a huge gob of llama spit all the way up from his third stomach. It hit Neil full on the chest like a very messy paintball. Neil staggered backwards, blundering into Luke and Jason and knocking them off their feet.

The train drew very slowly away from the platform. The panting, shaky Warriors stared out of the window, silently begging the driver to pick up speed.

Just two carriages down, another face stared out.

Tony Catchpole had intended to get out here. This was his stop. Eatwell. Where the sheep had rescued the boy. But he wasn't getting out now. The sheep were on the train with him. He stood rooted. He hadn't imagined their leaping on-board any more than he was imagining the llama drama being played out on the platform. While Saffron hurled herself again and again at the departing train and Luke and Jason struggled to their feet, a disgusted Neil was examining his spit-spattered designer jacket.

'The answer,' said Lama Glama before trotting away, 'is grass, corn silage and a discarded satsuma.'

The three humans left on the platform glared at each other.

'You've made me miss my train,' said Jason crossly. He whistled for Saffron. 'Heel, girl. Heel!'

The disappointed dog ignored his command and continued to run up and down the platform, barking excitedly. Neil stood for a moment, staring at her, and Luke realised, with a sinking heart, that he was having another of his 'brilliant ideas'.

'The dog,' Neil asked sharply. 'Is it any good?'

Jason hesitated. 'Yes,' he replied. 'Very good. Why?'

'How much d'you want for it?' Neil was taking his wallet from his back pocket.

Jason did some quick calculations. The pet shop in Loch Glooming would give him around fifty pounds if he was lucky.

'Four hundred pounds,' he said firmly.

'Two hundred,' retorted Neil.

'Three hundred,' said Jason.

'Done!' Neil slapped the last of his cash into Jason's hand.

Jason felt a twinge of guilt. But only a very small one. He hadn't exactly told this town guy a lie. Saffron *was* a good dog. She just wasn't a good sheepdog. Besides, Jason's TV was broken. Three hundred pounds would buy him a nice new one.

Neil turned to Luke. 'Well don't just stand there,' he ordered. 'Go get our dog.' He turned back to Jason. 'Where's that train going?' he demanded rudely.

'North. It doesn't stop again till it gets to Loch Glooming.'

'When's the next one?'

'Monday.'

Neil started to chew his fingernails, not sure what to do.

Jason decided to be helpful. 'Is that yellow car in the lane yours?' he asked.

Neil stopped chewing. 'What if it is?' he said suspiciously.

Jason shrugged. 'If it's as fast as it looks, you might just get to Loch Glooming before the train. The road runs beside the railway.'

Neil grinned. Things were looking up.

'Nasty brutes, llamas,' Jason observed, nodding at Neil's jacket. 'Give me sheep any day.'

But Neil had already turned and was running towards the station exit. Luke was crouching in front of the dog, trying to persuade her to stand up. She had tired of chasing the train and didn't want to move again.

'Her name's Saffron,' called Jason. Then, still in helpful mood, he added: 'She likes crisps.'

Luke felt in the pocket of his parka. There were a few soggy crisps amongst the fluff and scraps of paper at the bottom. He held them out to Saffron. She sniffed, thought about it, then snaffled them up.

'Good girl,' cooed Luke. 'Now follow me. Nice dog. Nice Saffron.'

Maybe it was his pleading tone or maybe it was the damp crisps. Saffron stood up, wagged her tail and followed Luke to the car.

'Bye, old girl,' called Jason, folding his money as she trotted away. 'Be good!'

'You get in first,' said Neil hastily to Luke, noting the dog's dirty paws. 'It can sit on your lap.'

13
Tony's Train Ride

Looking back through the window of the slowly moving train, Wills watched the three humans for a moment but then, as the train picked up speed, something else caught his eye. Sitting in a field beside the railway line was a strange blue object with long, blade-like things on top. And beside it were some different humans.

'Look!' cried Wills, 'Isn't that Tod and Ida – over there by the blue thing?'

The others crowded around the window, but the field was slipping quickly past now and they only got a glimpse.

'Couldn't have been, dear,' said Sal. 'We're such a long way North now.'

'No,' agreed Wills. 'No. I suppose not.'

There was an uncomfortable silence. It was the

first time any of them had thought about Tod and Ida since the quest began. They suddenly felt guilty about that.

'They'll be sooo upset we've gone,' said Jaycey.

The others agreed.

'We will go back, won't we?' said Oxo. 'I mean, when we've done the business with the Baaton, and Aries rules again and everything. We will go back to the farm?'

'Of course, of course,' promised Sal soothingly.

'Good,' said Oxo. 'Only I do miss cauliflower night.'

The train moved on, gathering speed as it went, and the sheep turned their thoughts to where to settle for the next part of their journey.

Back in the field beside the railway, Tod and Ida stood next to the helicopter and stretched their legs. Far from being able to see for miles as Ida had hoped, they'd been able to see nothing at all from the air. It had finally got too dangerous to fly in the thick mist and the landing was even more hairy. They'd only just missed the railway as they came down. Lady Babcott got out and stood beside them.

'Sorry we've been forced down,' she said. 'Still, this *is* Eatwell, where your sheep were filmed rescuing the little boy from the railway line. I guess they must be somewhere very close.'

'Oh, we can't thank you enough,' said Gran, who was still bubbling with excitement after her helicopter ride. She tucked her arm into Lady Babcott's and they all marched off into the mist.

'Wills . . . Jaycey . . .' Gran called. 'Oxo, Links, Sal . . . Where are you?'

Tod followed, peering from side to side, wishing he had a torch to penetrate the mist. One of those head torches would be useful. He thought briefly of the men in Gran's field and wondered if they'd found their mobile phone yet.

On the train, the Warriors had finally settled into the guard's van. There was no food here but a bit more space for them to spread out. Sal couldn't remember what verse of the Songs of the Fleece she had got up to, so was just about to begin from the beginning again when a voice made her jump.

'Tickets, please!'

The ticket inspector was standing in the doorway, looking very grumpy. Unticketed livestock were a serious offence.

'No ticket, no ride,' he said. Then, when no one spoke: 'All right, we'll make an unscheduled stop and turf you all off.'

'No, don't do that. I'll pay for them,' said another voice hastily. 'They're with me.'

The sheep blinked. Standing behind the ticket inspector was Tony Catchpole. Wills wondered again if he was seeing things. First Tod and Ida, now Tony. But it definitely was him. Tony paid for the tickets, then bought the entire stock of food and drinks from the snacks trolley and spent the next three hours in the guard's van with the sheep. He knew each of them by name and chatted about Eppingham and Tod and Ida, just to make them feel comfortable.

But all the time, Tony himself was bursting with excitement. He was trying to spot signs that they'd been modified by aliens. And he was puzzled that he couldn't find any. Their eyes weren't glazed, they didn't seem disturbed. They just munched crisps and chocolate fingers and slurped the tea he poured into the fire bucket for them. Then he looked again at the thing hanging around Jaycey's neck. He tried to get closer but the sheep wouldn't let him.

'Baaton . . . Baaton . . . Baaton . . .' they bleated.

It didn't make sense that they would be carrying an ordinary mobile phone. It had to be something else. Then he realised what and became even more excited.

'It must be a receiver!' he told the sheep. 'So the aliens can control you. I bet they're controlling you right now!'

He knelt down by the window so that he could peer up at the sky directly above, in case the UFO was close overhead. The sheep watched with interest and looked to Wills for an explanation of this odd human behaviour. Wills shrugged.

'No idea,' he admitted. 'I think he's a bit batty.'

Tony got a crick in the neck but he didn't see any UFOs. What he did see, though, confused and rather worried him.

There was a main road beside the railway, sharing the same valley floor as it wound northwards. A yellow sports car was scorching its tyres as it sped along the road. Sometimes the train was a little in front, sometimes the car overtook and gained the lead for a few minutes. It appeared to be some kind of race. A very dangerous one for the people in the car, Tony thought. And he tried to remember where he'd seen a car like that before. It was at Eppingham. On the night the sheep had been abducted. The night he'd given Nisha a daffodil. The car was in the lead now and streaking away.

Tony turned his attention back to the sheep.

'We shall shortly be arriving at Loch Glooming,' announced the train tannoy. 'Loch Glooming is the next and final stop. Please leave the train, taking all your personal belongings with you.'

'And your sheep,' added the voice of the cross ticket inspector.

Tony scrambled to his feet and fumbled for his mobile phone.

'Hello, Cousin Angus? It's Tony again. Did you manage to sort something for me . . .? Yes, I know I only gave you a couple of hours but any old truck will do . . . Great . . . See you in a few minutes.'

He glanced at the sheep and moved away before making his second call, his cheeks turning rather pink as it was answered.

The Warriors had lost interest in Tony now and were gazing through the windows at the scenery. They could see mountains in the near distance. North was close. The land of the Soay sheep.

'We are coming, great Aries,' murmured Sal. 'Your Warriors are coming . . .'

The train drew to a halt.

'Stay here,' ordered Tony, and he jumped out on to the platform, closed the train door behind him and hurried off.

'We's on a quest, man,' Links called after him. 'We don't stay nowhere, innit.'

'No way,' agreed Oxo. He led the way out of the guard's van into the corridor and butted the door Tony had closed. Nothing happened.

'Try the button?' suggested Wills. 'Up there.'

Oxo stood on his hind legs and butted the 'Door Open' button. The door hissed sideways and the Warriors jumped out.

'Exit to town this way,' indicated Wills, reading a sign. 'I expect that's what we want.' And he turned and trotted away. Straight into a trap.

14
Saffron Strikes

The yellow car had screeched to a halt outside the station, minutes before the train had arrived. Neil had jumped out of the driver's seat and Saffron had bounded off Luke's lap. Now she stood beside Luke, wagging her tail, hoping for more damp crisps.

Neil took control. 'Heel, dog,' he ordered. He positioned himself just outside the station exit. Saffron ran to his side, then crouched low, expectant and eager. Perhaps he had crisps too.

Passengers poured out past them.

Wills and the other Warriors didn't hear Neil's whistle until they were outside the station. Then it was too late. The dog was in their faces, and at their heels and tails. Everywhere, in fact, that a sheepdog can get, and all at the same time. Saffron was having a sheep moment. These were very rare. About once a

122

year, which was why she had been sold. Train, car and bicycle chasing moments were much more common.

'That'll do!' ordered Neil firmly. 'Move 'em now. This way!'

He whistled again and before the terrified, bewildered Warriors could gather their wits, they were being herded swiftly away from the station, away from the town. The dog swirled around them with bared teeth, giving Oxo no chance to butt.

Luke was very impressed by Neil's exhibition of shepherding.

'I didn't know you could whistle like that,' he said admiringly.

Neil smirked and prodded the sheep nearest to him with a stick he'd picked up from the roadside.

'Easy,' he said. 'You just have to show the dog who's boss.'

'So, uh, where are we going?' asked Luke, running to keep up.

'Away from prying eyes,' said Neil. He tossed the stick to Luke. 'Take over. And as soon as we're out of this grotty town, stop the dog and get the phone. I'll be right behind.'

Luke fumbled on the ground for the stick he had failed to catch.

'Er, right,' he said, looking anxiously at Saffron, who was yapping excitedly and running in ever faster circles around the frightened sheep.

Meanwhile, Tony was feeling very let down. His Cousin Angus had promised a truck – any old truck. Instead, he was waiting behind the station with a tractor. True, it had a trailer. But the trailer was full of manure and straw. There was hardly room in it for five very special sheep.

'Best I could do, laddie,' Angus said. 'Couldn't get the truck started. Take it or leave it.'

Tony took it. 'Thanks, Angus. I'll return it a.s.a.p.'

He shook hands with Angus then ran back to the train.

'No . . .!' he wailed when he saw the open door and the empty guard's van. He ran out of the station again and looked wildly around. In the distance, he could see the sheep being driven away from town by a very excitable dog and a scruffy guy in a dirty parka. Following them slowly along the road was the yellow car he'd seen from the train window. He breathed a sigh of relief. Not aliens this time. Human thieves. He could deal with *them*. He raced back to the tractor, scrambled into the driver's seat, revved the engine and headed after the yellow car, his trailer full of manure and straw bouncing along behind.

The sheep were being driven south. Away from the North and the mountains where they would surely find Aries. Their quest had been halted and there was nothing they could do. Wills hung his head in shame.

'I'm so sorry, guys,' he said. Then he wept like a lamb. 'I'm so sorry. It's all my fault. I should have looked where I was going as we came off the train.'

'We've failed you, great Aries,' wailed Sal through her own tears. 'We *all* should have looked.'

'Yeah, we's supposed to be Warriors, innit,' said Links angrily.

'Ohmygrass,' whimpered Jaycey. 'Does this mean Aries will die and Lambad will eat us for breakfast?'

'Give over,' muttered Oxo. ' We're not finished yet.'

But then the dog nipped his heels hard and he had to run with the others.

Behind the flock, Neil was having trouble driving

so slowly. They were out of the town now and as soon as the tractor behind him turned off, he would yell at Luke to stop. He drummed his fingers impatiently on the steering wheel. Then his phone rang. He snatched it up.

It was his tracker mate again and Neil was less than polite.

'Thanks a bunch!' he snarled ungratefully into his mobile. 'I know it's in Loch Glooming. I can see it!'

This wasn't precisely true because the sheep had just rounded a bend in the road in front of him. Anxious not to lose sight of them, Neil accelerated as he took the bend. He misjudged it and went up the verge and down again, his foot still on the accelerator.

'Now look what you've made me do!' he screamed into the phone before tossing it aside and grabbing the steering wheel with both hands. But he was too late. The car had slewed around and was careering sideways into the flock.

By the time it had come to a juddering halt and Luke and Saffron had got out of the ditch, the sheep had disappeared.

15
Deep in the Doody

Tony Catchpole was not a fool. He had followed the yellow car and seen it plough into the flock. From his seat, high in the tractor cab, he had also seen the sheep leaping through the scrubby line of trees beside the road. And he had quickly turned his tractor down the slope after them.

As the sheep gathered together at the bottom of the slope, they could hear the barking of the dog and the angry shouts of the two men on the road above.

'Ohmygrass, ohmygrass . . . What do we do now?' whimpered Jaycey.

'Hope the dog keeps barking,' said Wills. 'It'll stop when it's picked up our scent again.'

They heard a grinding, jolting noise and stumbled around to see a tractor heading towards them through the dense bracken. With Tony Catchpole at the wheel. The tractor pulled up, Tony leapt out, ran to the end of the trailer and began letting the tailboard down.

'Get in . . .! Get in . . .!' he whispered.

He gestured vigorously at them. The Warriors looked at each other. Was this some kind of trick? To do with UFOs, whatever they were? Suddenly the dog stopped barking. The sheep leapt and scrabbled rapidly up into the trailer. As they did so, Tony grabbed up a pitchfork and began dragging a covering of straw and manure over them.

'Keep still and keep quiet,' he begged as he pitched smelly load after smelly load over their heads. When they were completely hidden, he lifted the tailboard and shoved the rusty bolts into place. Then he ran back to the tractor, climbed in and started up again. He drove back up through the bracken, over the ditch and out on to the stony road. Just in front of the yellow sports car.

Neil and Luke turned and stared.

'Hey!' shouted Neil. 'Hey!' And he ran after the tractor.

He overtook it and waved at Tony to halt. Tony

pulled up but didn't turn off the engine.

'Did you see any sheep down there?' yelled Neil, above the noise.

'Och, no,' yelled back Tony, risking a Scottish accent.

He gave a little wave and drove off at a scorching five miles an hour. But before they were out of sight, the trailer hit a bump and as it did so, the ends of two delicate horns poked up through the manure. Neil blinked.

'We've been had!' he snarled.

He raced back to the sports car. 'Well, come on!' he shouted at Luke. 'He's got our sheep!'

Luke bundled into the car after him. Saffron bounded in too and sat on Luke's lap.

In the tractor's wing mirror, Tony saw the yellow car suddenly take off after him. He didn't know who the men were, or why they wanted Ida White's sheep, and he didn't really care. He found a hammer under his seat.

'Get ready to rock 'n' roll!' he shouted, though the sheep couldn't hear him. Then he whacked the throttle with the hammer. The tractor positively leapt forward. Ten miles an hour, at least. Deep in the manure and straw, Links was rapping.

'Don't mess with the Posse
Cos we's real moody,
Even though it's us who's
Now in the doody . . .'

Despite the twisty-turniness of the road, which had become no more than a track wending its way between the pine trees, the sports car quickly caught up with the tractor. There was no room to overtake but Neil drove close behind, blaring his horn and yelling out of his window.

'Hold on to your fleeces!' yelled Tony, and he swung the tractor violently right, on to an even narrower and bumpier track through the trees, with pot holes the size of moon craters.

'Ohmygrass, ohmyteeth . . .!' Jaycey's jaws snapped and shook. Her third and fourth stomachs collided.

The sports car didn't like the pot holes either. Neil was forced to slow down and soon the tractor disappeared round a bend.

Once out of sight, Tony jumped down from his tractor cab and joined the sheep in the trailer.

'Get up to the tractor end and hang on tight!' he shouted excitedly, forgetting that sheep don't have much to hang on with. He shooed them right away from the tailboard, then jumped to the ground again and stood watching the bend in the road. The Warriors, crammed beyond the mountain of manure and straw, saw the car appear round the bend. They saw Tony unbolt the tailboard of the trailer and heard a clang as it dropped down. They saw Tony run back to the cab, and heard a dong as he hit something with his hammer. Then they heard a hissing whine and the floor beneath them began to tilt. On Angus Catchpole's ancient tractor, the only thing that worked well was the hydraulic system.

'Ohmygrass . . .' wailed Jaycey.

'Ohmystomachs,' gasped Sal.

They both hung on to Oxo with their teeth, but even he couldn't stop himself sliding slowly after the manure, down towards the open end of the trailer, taking Links and Wills with him too.

In the car, Neil realised what was about to happen

but had no time to reverse. He could only watch in horror as a ton of straw and muck slid from the trailer towards him. Then his gleaming pride and joy was buried beneath a steaming dung heap and he could see nothing.

Tony whacked the control lever in the tractor cab again, just as the Warriors were about to slide out with the last of the manure. The trailer floor began to level out once more and they were able to scrabble away from the edge.

'Stay back!' yelled Tony at the sheep as he returned to the trailer to slam the tailboard shut. By the time Neil and Luke had forced the sports car doors open and struggled out, he was back in his tractor cab again.

'Och, sorry aboot that,' he called. 'I didnae see you so close behind me.' He waved cheerily and drove off.

When the tractor and trailer had lurched out of sight around the next corner, he shouted at his passengers.

'Well done, sheep. Let's go!'

He drove on, whistling to himself, while the Warriors shook the mucky debris from their fleeces and wondered where exactly they were going *to*.

Neil knew he'd been made a fool of.

'Don't just stare at it, then!' he shouted at Luke. 'They're getting away. Dig!'

Then his phone rang. He checked the caller's identity. It was the Very Nasty Boss again. He decided not to answer. Digging dung with his bare hands was preferable.

16
No Escape

Back in Yorkshire, Tod and Ida had searched the hillside near the railway station for hours, and found nothing except a llama sitting humming to itself.

'Never mind, Gran,' said Tod. 'There's lots more hills yet.'

'That's the trouble,' said Gran, sounding tired and, for the first time, a bit depressed. 'There's too many of them.'

Then, through the clearing mist, they saw Lady Babcott striding uphill to meet them.

'You'll never guess,' she panted. 'The man at the railway station says five sheep got on the train we saw. Come on. Back to the chopper. They'll be at Loch Glooming by now!'

*

Tony Catchpole was also heading for Loch Glooming. He was doubling back towards the station, hoping Cousin Angus wouldn't mind about the missing manure.

Tony was happy. Very happy. His second call on the train had been to Nisha Patel, and Nisha had agreed to meet him at Loch Glooming Station. Now that he had the sheep, Tony could show Organic TV how the poor animals had been modified by aliens. He could point out to the world the electronic collar by which they were being controlled. He could give Nisha another daffodil.

Then, without warning, the smoke-belching roar of the tractor's engine became a feeble phut-phut, and the tractor and trailer rolled gently to a halt. Tony peered at the fuel gauge. The needle was pointing to Empty. He bashed it with the hammer. Still empty. His happiness evaporated. He pulled out his phone to call Nisha and explain that he would be late. But he was out of phone battery as well as tractor fuel. If he wanted to meet her at the station, he would have to run. Fast.

In the trailer, the Warriors could hear Tony

muttering to himself as he jumped down from his seat. They watched him leap the fence into a nearby field and haul up an armful of withered greenery. He hurried back and tossed it into the trailer.

'Just stay here, yes?' he pleaded. 'Stay here. I won't be long. I'll come back with Nisha and some petrol and you'll be really famous. Yes? Good. Good sheep.' And he ran off.

'What's Nisha?' asked Oxo, when Tony had disappeared. 'Some kind of nice grub?' He nosed the withered greenery, which turned out to be the limp remains of last season's Brussels sprouts. 'Because no way am I eating *this*.'

'I don't know 'bout Nisha,' said Links. 'But what if he don't come back, man, and those other dudes show up?'

'What if he *does* come back?' said Sal. 'Surely we should take a chance now. We all saw the mountains. North is close. What are we waiting for?'

'Er, Oxo, I think,' said Wills.

'Waste not, want not,' mumbled the Oxford piously through a mouthful of mildewed sprouts.

Then he followed the others as one by one they

jumped out of the trailer on to a springy patch of roadside heather and headed north again.

A long way behind them, the yellow sports car, now a blotched khaki brown, had been mostly excavated from the dung heap.

'Right,' said Neil, 'let's see if we can shift it. I'll get in, you push.'

'Why don't you call the phone tracker guy first?' asked Luke. 'That tractor could be anywhere by now.'

Neil didn't answer.

'You've upset him, haven't you?' said Luke.

'Just shut up and start pushing,' snapped Neil.

He dabbed at the keypad on his mobile.

'Who *are* you calling, then?' asked Luke.

'The sheep, of course.'

Luke stared. 'The sheep?' he said faintly.

Neil stared back. 'Because the guy on the tractor who's got them will answer, won't he, nerdbrain. Maybe we can do a deal.'

Trotting North, Jaycey suddenly skittered sideways.

'Ohmygrass . . . Ohmygrass . . .'

The other Warriors heard the noise and quickly gathered round.

'Ohmygrassohmygrassohmygrass . . .!'

'Don't be upset, dear,' said Sal soothingly. 'Hearing the voice of Aries so close is a daunting experience.'

Sal took the plastic bag in her mouth to muffle the awe-inspiring sound and as she did so her teeth pressed the answer button. Instantly, the sound stopped. There was a moment's silence, then they heard a voice. To Sal's astonishment it sounded human.

'Hullo? Hullo? Can you hear me?' It paused. 'Say something, then.'

Sal let go of the Baaton bag and it banged against Jaycey's chest. Sal didn't understand why Aries should be addressing them in human speech but she felt she must reply.

'Baa . . .'

'Say again?'

'Baa . . .' repeated Sal.

The other Warriors gathered round.

'Listen,' said the voice of the Baaton. 'I'd like to offer you a deal.'

Sal didn't know what a deal was.

'Baa . . . Baa . . .' she answered respectfully.

'Stop messing around and name your price.'

She didn't know what a price was either.

'Baa . . . Baa . . . Baa . . .'

The Warriors crowded closer. They could all now hear a bewildered whispering from the Baaton.

'He's talking like a sheep. All he says is "Baa . . .". It's really spooky.'

'Baa . . .' replied Sal. And then the other Warriors joined in.

'Baa . . . Baa . . . Baa.'

'Take it or leave it. This is your last chance . . .'

Wills stiffened. He knew that a last chance was not a good thing. And something else was worrying him. The voice was vaguely familiar, though he couldn't think why.

'I think Aries is telling us to hurry,' he said, and he quickly closed his teeth around the bag and the Baaton.

The voice stopped and Wills led the way onwards, feeling confused and suddenly rather frightened.

Neil stood staring at his phone.

'He's rung off.' He pulled an angry face, then stuffed the phone back into his pocket. 'But they can't be that far ahead.' He put his shoulder to the back of the car to heave it out of the last of the manure. 'Come on, come on!' He gestured for Luke to take over and ran round to the driver's seat. The engine roared, the wheels spun and Luke got covered in a flying brown spray before the tyres finally gripped.

'Here, mind my upholstery!' shouted Neil as he saw the state Luke was in.

Luke was beyond caring about Neil's upholstery. He got in beside him and wiped his sleeve on the white leather seat. Saffron didn't mind the mess. Or the stink. She jumped in after Luke and sat on his lap, wagging her tail and licking his filthy face.

The car bounced and lurched along painfully for a while, then the unmade lane rejoined the main track and they were able to go faster. Soon they saw what they were looking for.

'Tractor's up ahead!' shouted Luke, feeling relieved. He had changed his mind again about giving himself up. He would get the phone from the little sheep before Neil could, then he would run straight to the police in Loch Glooming. *They* could divert the money back to its rightful owners.

On reaching the tractor, Luke jumped out of the car before Neil had finished braking. But the trailer was empty. There was no sign of the driver or of the sheep. Luke slumped down in the middle of the road and put his head in his hands.

'What are you doing?' bawled Neil. 'Get back in the car. They've got to be really, really close!'

He jumped back in and Luke, feeling he had no choice, followed. Saffron was already there, feet on the dashboard, excited. Neil drove on, steering with one hand, the other arm resting on the open window frame as he scanned the fields around. A few eager minutes later, he shouted again.

'There they are, look!'

He was right. The sheep were milling about further along the narrow track, where it passed between a high stone wall on one side and a rocky outcrop on the other.

'Bionic?' laughed Neil. 'Super intelligent? No way.' And he punched the air.

'Why've they stopped?' Luke asked. 'There's no gate or anything.'

'Don't know, don't care,' replied Neil. 'They're just stupid woolbags.' He savoured the moment. 'Let the dog out, and we've got them.'

17
The North

The Rare Breed Warriors had been halted by the widest cattle grid they had ever seen. It was there to stop farm animals from straying into the thick pine forest beyond. Its smooth rounded bars seemed to grin up at the sheep, as if knowing they dared not step on it. Livestock won't tread on a grid for fear of getting hooves trapped between the bars.

The rock face to their right was too steep to climb. The wall to their left too high to jump. And the dog and the men who had tried to trap them in London were racing towards them. The dog was barking. They could almost feel its hot breath on their backs.

'Ohmygrass . . .' whimpered Jaycey. 'We're trappedtrappedtrapped!'

Links didn't think so.

'Let's roll, man!' he suddenly shouted.

'This is no time for one of your moves,' bleated Sal. Then to her astonishment, Links threw himself sideways on the grid, kicked his feet in the air and began to do just what he'd said: roll.

Wills instantly followed. Then all the sheep were on the grid, rolling and wriggling across it on their backs.

'Go dog! Go!' yelled Neil, but Saffron was going nowhere. She only barked even more ferociously, to cover up her own dread of stepping on the slippery, gappy bars. She just couldn't do it. And her sheep moment was fading quickly.

Neil and Luke ran back to the car and Saffron jumped on to Luke's lap again.

'Why didn't you show her who's boss?' asked Luke, as they trundled slowly over the grid. Neil ignored him.

'Chuck her out,' he snapped, as soon as they were on the other side.

Luke opened the door and nudged Saffron until she had to jump.

'Go on, you big wimp!' Neil shouted at her. 'I paid three hundred quid for you! Prove you're not completely useless.'

'She's not a wimp,' retorted Luke. 'She's sensitive.'

Saffron ran after the disappearing sheep and Neil drove as fast as he could along the winding track after her. He caught up with her standing at a stream at the edge of the forest.

Neil drove straight past the dog and through the stream.

'What's the matter?' he called mockingly back at Saffron, as spray from the wheels soaked her. 'Don't like getting your feet wet? Which way now, Superdog?'

Saffron suddenly became agitated, barking towards the wide track in front of the car. The track was straight and steep, cutting uphill through the forest, dividing it in two. It was rutted with wheel marks, for this was a forest where the pine trees were grown and cut down for timber. There was a pile of logs at the top of the hill, and, struggling up towards it, were the sheep.

'Yes!' shouted Neil, punching the air again. He drove rapidly on to the wide forest track, revved the engine hard and started up the slope after the sheep.

'Go get 'em!' he yelled at Saffron. But Saffron stayed where she was. She stopped barking and watched uneasily as the car roared and bumped up the hill. The sheep were suddenly nowhere to be seen. Where had they gone?

Hiding behind the pile of logs at the top, Jaycey panicked when she heard the low grinding roar coming towards her.

'Ohmygrass! The beastthebeastthebeast . . .!'

'What beast? What beast?' asked all the other sheep, turning to Jaycey in alarm.

'How do I know?' she bleated. 'All forests have beasts, don't they? That's what my mum said.'

'Jaycey, it's the car, remember?' said Wills, trying to calm her down.

'Car! Car! Car!' cried Jaycey. One reason to panic was as good as another.

'Shush, I've got a plan,' said Wills. He turned and spoke rapidly to the others. They nodded in agreement. They had to act as one and act fast.

But Jaycey was too frightened to listen to Wills. She dashed out from behind the pile of logs and was instantly transfixed by the two great yellow eyes coming towards her.

Neil had just flicked on his headlights and there it

was, all lit up: the black-and-white sheep with the phone in the plastic bag swinging from its petrified neck.

'Got you this time, woolbag!' he shouted exultantly.

'Don't run it over, then!' cried Luke.

'Why not?' laughed Neil. 'Can't bite or butt if it's squidged.'

The Warriors didn't hear this nasty threat. Their heads were down, waiting for the word from Oxo.

'One, two, three . . . Butt!' he cried, then smashed his great forehead into the pile of logs. The others did the same. 'And again!' cried Oxo. 'Butt! Butt! Butt!'

Neil stared. The logs piled next to the black-and-white sheep suddenly ceased to be a pile. A few bounced off. The ones at the bottom began to slide. Then the whole lot started to roll downhill, towards the car.

'Reverse! Reverse!' screamed Luke helpfully.

Neil did so, fast, but it's hard to steer backwards downhill pursued by half a forest. One wheel left the track, then another; then the car slid sideways and ended in a ditch, right way up but stuck fast. The logs rumbled by, casually denting the roof and doors as they went. The forest fell silent.

'Are you all right, Neil?' ventured Luke anxiously.

'Wonderful, mate,' came the reply. 'Absolutely socking wonderful . . .'

'Look,' said Luke. 'Sheep.'

Neil slowly raised his head.

Luke was right. A huddle of the woolbags was standing above them, floodlit by the remaining headlight beam. If Neil hadn't known better, he could have sworn they looked concerned. Guilty, almost.

'Don't worry,' he shouted at them savagely. 'The car's a write-off but we're just fine. Really comfy.'

The Warriors looked at each other.

Wills shrugged. 'I suppose that's all right then,' he said.

'Yeah,' said Oxo. 'What's a write-off?'

Wills didn't know. But the important thing was the plan had worked. The car wouldn't be chasing them any further.

Luke shivered, and not just because of the plummeting temperature. He was scared. He didn't like forests. Saffron hadn't exactly proved useful to them but he was glad when she bounded up and squeezed into the car again.

A noise overhead made him duck. When he risked looking up, he saw only a helicopter. If it had looked like a police helicopter he would have got out of the car and waved his arms and shouted. But it didn't. At least, he didn't think the police used bright blue helicopters. He slid further down into the not-so-white leather seat and put his arms around Saffron's warm body.

The sheep also heard the loud noise in the sky and hurried from the track into the shelter of the trees.

'Hey . . .' Oxo stared upwards in amazement. 'Did you see the size of that mosquito?'

In the helicopter, Tod and Ida gazed down at the purple blackness of the pine forest but didn't see the sheep. It was an unlikely place for sheep to go, in any case, but there'd been no sign of them back at Loch Glooming or on the rugged open ground near the town.

Then Tod saw a car. It seemed to be very badly parked. In a ditch. He urgently tapped his gran's hand and pointed.

'Look, Gran,' he said. 'That car. It's like the yellow one those guys in our field had.'

Gran looked. 'Could be,' she said. 'A bit mucky

now, though.' She laughed. 'I wonder if his precious upholstery's still white.'

Lady Babcott's voice crackled in their headsets. 'No sign of your sheep?' she asked.

'No. Only a car we thought we recognised,' said Tod.

The helicopter banked away.

'OK,' said Lady Babcott. 'We'll land at the town and make enquiries.'

Down in the forest, with the sound of the giant mosquito fading, Oxo was anxious to move on.

'Come on, sheep, let's ship out.' He really didn't fancy pine needles for supper.

The sun was almost down and Sal glimpsed its redness through the trees.

'Remind me, dear,' she said to Wills, 'Turn which way at the sunset?'

'Right,' said Links. He began humming his latest rap.

'Right on to the right,
Cos the Eppingham Posse

Is headin' for a fight.

We's bringin' home the Baaton

After all the way we come,

And if we meet the Lambad,

We's gonna bite him on the –'

'Yes, thank you, Links,' said Sal hastily. 'I think we have a way to go yet.'

'Way to go,' agreed Links, nodding. 'Way to go . . .'

They continued uphill until the forest finally thinned and the ground levelled off. A freezing wind rushed to meet them, and they stood for a moment, blinking and gazing across a narrow strip of boggy ground towards the mountains. The bog and rocks merged gently into the foothills, but rising above these gentle slopes were rock faces wider, steeper and sharper than anything any of them had ever imagined. None of them spoke but they all felt scared. Very scared. In front of the Warriors stood a sign:

WELCOME TO THE NORTH.
HAVE YOU:

- Told your next of kin where you are?

- Told your next of kin when you will be back?
- Told your next of kin what's for dinner?
- Made a will?
- Donned appropriate foul-weather clothing?
- Brought someone to carry it for you if it gets too hot?

The sheep couldn't answer yes to any of the questions, with the possible exception of foul-weather clothing. The biting wind made them doubt even that. Above them, the pale-green sky was turning dark grey.

'So this is it, then,' said Wills. 'The land of the Soays.'

'Yeah, man,' said Links, his teeth chattering. 'Where the weakest p-p-perish, innit.'

'Ohmyg-g-grass . . .' whimpered Jaycey.

'What if the Golden Horn Dude ain't here after all?' asked Links.

'He'll be here,' said Sal with certainty. 'And there's not a minute to lose. He's been without his life-giving Baaton for much too long.'

'Onwards and upwards!' cried Oxo. And he hurried on before his hooves froze.

One by one, the other sheep nodded and lowered

their heads against the wind, and the Rare Breed Warriors marched on determinedly towards the now-glowering mountains.

They were almost at the foothills when, without warning, Jaycey squealed and hurled herself to the ground.

'Ohmygrassohmygrass . . .' she gurgled, her face in the frozen dirt.

'What's the matter with her now?' asked Oxo.

Jaycey was twitching a front hoof in the vague direction of the sky. The other sheep looked up and saw winged black dots circling high above.

'Crows! Crows! Crows!' bleated Jaycey. Her mum had told her all about those as well; how they pecked naughty lambs' eyes out.

'They won't hurt you, dear,' Sal reassured her. 'Truly, they won't.'

'No way, man,' agreed Links. 'Crows is sweet, innit.'

But he wasn't as sure as he sounded. None of them was. This was the North, where the weakest perished.

'Jaycey, remember what we've faced already,' said Wills. 'The Tube, The Eye. The Grid. Remember how brave you've been. You're a Warrior Sheep. You're not

153

going to let a few crows stop us saving the Ram of Rams, are you?'

They nudged Jaycey to her feet and plodded on.

The sun had set now, but the dark sky became strangely lighter. Sleet began to fall, stinging their eyes as the wind drove it towards them. And as the ground rose higher, so did the wind; and the sleet turned to snow.

The Warriors arranged themselves in single file, Oxo in the lead, his great head defying the blizzard as they struggled forward. They could no longer see the mountain peaks, no longer see anything through the whipping whiteness except the Warrior directly in front of them; could no longer hear anything above the shrieking wind.

On either side of them, the snow was settling despite the wind. Already drifts were forming, hiding dips and hollows in the ground. Ice caked the Warriors' faces, freezing their eyelids shut.

'Ohmygrass . . .' sobbed Jaycey. 'Where are you, Oxo!'

Oxo didn't hear. He had stumbled and was struggling chest-deep through a drift.

'We must stick close together!' called Wills, but his voice was lost, ripped away in the storm. He could see no one in front of him now, and when he managed to turn, he could see no one behind him, either.

The snow was up to his chest. Then his neck. He stretched upwards, desperately straining to keep his nose free. To breathe. But the snow did not relent. It covered his eyes; it covered his head. Wills disappeared beneath the whiteness.

18
Kraw

By dawn, the blizzard had blown itself out. A smooth white blanket of snow covered every inch of the foothills and was drawn up snugly around the base of the mountains. The icy peaks glistened in the early sun. It was a beautiful scene. But deadly. For the snow was deep as well as smooth, and every Warrior was buried beneath it. Only the warmth of their faint breathing kept them alive, melting enough snow around their muzzles to create tiny pockets of air. Soon though, their bodies and lungs would be frozen solid and the breathing would stop.

Jaycey was the first to be aware of movement above her: a jabbing sound, as if someone or something was digging in the snow. Then something glanced against her left horn. Something hard and sharp. A beak! It clattered against her horns again, left then right.

'Ohmygrass!' Jaycey's head was suddenly free. Freezing air tore into her rapidly expanding lungs. She gulped in more air. 'Ohmy . . .' Sharp claws dug roughly into her fleece.

'Kraa! Kraa! Kraa!'

More claws pricked her flesh and she felt herself being hauled upwards, dragged from the heavy grip of the snow. She could see the frozen ground beneath her dangling hooves and, looking up, she could see black, shiny wings, dozens of them, all beating hard.

'Ohmygrassohmygrass . . . Crowscrowscrows . . .' she whimpered.

Suddenly, the claws released their grip and she fell back with a thud on to the soft snowy blanket. A mob of birds circled above her. Hooded crows? Carrion crows? They looked the same to her. And they all carried away lambs or pecked their eyes out. They hadn't carried her away so they must be settling for the eyes. She shut hers tight, too terrified even to faint.

Then a harsh voice croaked, close above her:

'Don't panic, love. Mountain Rescue.'

The muffled voices of the birds stirred Wills in his prison of snow. He strained upwards. He heard

157

a scratching noise, then something scrabbled at his woolly head, and he too could breathe. He saw Jaycey staggering to her feet. The Rescue Team crowded around him.

'How many more, mate?' asked their leader, whose name was Kraw. He spoke good ovine.

'Three,' gasped Wills.

He tried to remember where everyone had been when the blizzard had struck. Who'd been in front of whom. Links had been behind him. Wills nodded at the claw-patterned snow a few steps away.

'There,' he said. 'Try there.'

The crows dug in with their beaks and scraped with their claws. A head appeared with lumps of ice dangling from its curls.

'High in the North, man,
We is buried in the snow,
But the Warrior Sheeps
Is still go, go, go . . .'

'Actually, mate,' advised Kraw, 'I'd pipe down for a while.' He glanced at the snow-covered peaks of the towering mountains. 'No offence, voice-wise, but you don't want to start an avalanche.'

'Respect,' said Links, and shut up.

'You can still get out, though.'

'Oh,' said Links. 'Cool.' And he heaved the rest of himself out of the hole. 'Where's the Batterin' Ram?' he asked.

He soon saw. Oxo too had heard voices. A mini-eruption like an ice volcano showed the rescuers where to dig next.

'Survival rations?' he enquired hopefully as they dug him out.

'Sorry,' said Kraw. 'Nearest grub is back down in Glooming. Which is where you guys should be. It's strictly Soays only in the survival scenario up here.'

'Kraa! Kraa! Kraa!'

The calls of the rest of his team distracted him. Wills had led them to where he thought Sal might be, and they had made a breathing hole. Sal was deep down and sounded delirious.

'Aries . . .' she called. 'Is that you, Aries?'

'Uh, no, ma'm,' replied Kraw. 'I'm strictly Mountain Rescue.'

He nodded at his team and they resumed digging. Wills wriggled down and managed to burrow underneath Sal and push from below as she struggled out.

'Thank you, thank you,' she puffed. 'I've always said that crows are completely misunderstood.'

'Thank you, ma'm,' said Kraw. 'Maybe sheep aren't all brainless accidents waiting to happen, either.'

'Exactly,' agreed Sal. 'And one in particular is certainly not. The Soay that we seek. A wise and ancient ram with down-turned golden horns. Can you help us?'

Kraw thought for a moment.

'I don't know about the horns,' he said, 'but I saw an old one, right at the top, yesterday. He looked in pretty bad shape to me.'

'Where?' demanded Sal. 'Guide our hoofsteps.'

She lurched forward and the crows instinctively scuttled backwards, ready for emergency take-off.

'No way are you going up there,' said Kraw. 'You wouldn't last five minutes.'

'We must. We can't stop now!' cried Sal passionately. 'We are the Warrior Sheep, come to save Lord Aries. Show us the way. Please!'

Her yellow eyes were on fire. Kraw tried to hold her look but he wasn't used to stand-offs. The rescued usually said thank you, then went quietly back home.

For a few seconds, the only sound was the creaking plop of snow in the rescue holes. Then Kraw sighed.

'Go left over the rocks to avoid this deep snow. Then, when you reach the next flat bit, walk straight ahead. You'll pass a big barn. The path starts just behind it. Once you're on the path, don't deviate. It winds all the way up to Bony Peak. That's the summit. That's where I saw the sick old Soay yesterday.'

'Thank you,' breathed Sal. 'Thank you . . .'

Kraw took another step backwards. He was afraid she was going to kiss him.

'One thing you should know, if you're set on this,' he said. 'Humans use the Peak. They have a building at the very top. Some very strange and dangerous birds come out of there. It's a bad place.'

The wind was rising again. It tugged at the sheep's ice-stubbled fleeces.

'Good luck,' said Kraw shortly, breaking the silence. He nodded at his team, and with a flutter of wings, they were gone.

The Warriors stood quite still for a few more moments, then began scrambling across the slippery rocks in the direction Kraw had said. Towards Bony Peak.

'How about a rap, Links dear?' suggested Sal.

'Eh? The crow dude said no singin', innit.'

'I'm sure it'll be safe enough now,' said Sal. 'And we need a marching song. Aries may even hear us coming.'

Links shrugged then started nodding. And singing.

'We's the Eppingham Posse
An' we's goin' to the Peak
To find the lonesome Soay
And help him cos he's weak.
We ain't frightened of no shadows,
We ain't runnin' from no beak,
We is here to bring the Baaton,
Not to play no hide 'n' seek . . .'

'Yeah, man,' exclaimed Sal. 'Wicked jamming.'

The others took up the song too and marched on proudly towards their goal. So loud and brave were their voices that they didn't hear the helicopter.

*

Neil and Luke did. They were standing shivering in front of the WELCOME TO THE NORTH sign when they became aware of it high above them. Neil was shivering less than Luke because he'd forcibly swapped coats with him. Luke's parka was a bit warmer than his own jacket and it didn't stink of llama spit either. They'd spent an uncomfortable night in the wrecked car before fighting their way out and tramping up the snow-covered logging track. The forest had provided some shelter but here, in the open, the wind cut through Luke like a knife.

'We'll d-d-die up here,' he moaned.

'No, we won't,' snapped Neil. 'Not if we keep moving.' He peered into the distance, ignoring the helicopter. 'This white-out's gonna help us. The woolbags'll show up like chip grease on a tablecloth.' He stalked away.

Luke had heard of being snow-blind. Neil seemed to be going snow-mad. But it was slightly less cold walking behind him than standing by the WELCOME sign, so he followed.

'Are you coming?' he said to Saffron and felt happier when she wagged her tail and trotted along beside him. He glanced up at the helicopter hovering overhead and considered signalling to it. If only it *were* an unmarked police chopper. Prison would be so much warmer than this.

'Look!' Neil's excited voice cut through Luke's thoughts like the wind through his thin jacket. 'There!'

Luke squinted after the pointing finger, and saw the sheep. Neil had been right about one thing. They did show up like spots of chip grease against the pure white snow. They were in the foothills, heading for the highest crag.

'Come on!' urged Neil and he started to run.

In the helicopter overhead, there was also much excitement.

'There – look, Tod, there!' yelled Gran into her radio mike.

Tod punched the air and nodded vigorously. 'Yes!' he cried.

Lady Babcott's voice came through to them.

'Is it definitely them, dears?' she asked.

'I'd know them anywhere!' yelled back Gran.

Lady Babcott winced. She had given up asking Ida

not to shout into the mike. Then Tod's voice boomed in her ears. He was speaking to his grandmother.

'Look, Gran. Those two men running across the snow. They're the ones we saw in our paddock. The ones looking for their mobile phone.'

Gran looked and agreed. 'So it *was* their yellow car back there in the forest.'

'Weird, isn't it?' said Tod.

'No, I'm not sure it *is* weird,' yelled Gran after a moment. 'D'you know what I think? I think they're involved in the bank scam.'

Tod was startled. 'Why?' he asked.

'Because Jaycey's still got that plastic bag hanging round her neck. And I think the phone they're so desperate to find must be in it. That's why they're chasing her.'

'But what's that got to do with the bank?'

'Think about it, Tod,' yelled Gran. 'When did we first see those two oddballs? The night our money went missing. The same night they lost their phone.'

'So you reckon they somehow used the phone to steal the money from the bank?' said Tod.

Gran nodded vigorously. 'Yes. Then lost the phone.'

Tod was catching up now. 'And if it's still got some sort of evidence on it,' he said excitedly, 'data or stuff, they'd be mad keen to get it back.'

'What I can't figure out though,' said Gran, 'is how it got into our paddock. Or around Jaycey's neck.'

'No,' said Tod. 'And the other thing is that those two aren't exactly bright, are they? If you're right, I bet there's someone else involved in all this. A criminal mastermind.'

The helicopter tilted sharply sideways.

'Stand by for landing. Going down now.' Lady Babcott's voice suddenly sounded rather terse.

The Warriors had scrambled over the rocks and trotted past the big barn that Kraw had told them about. Now they were on the mountain path and struggling upwards. They were no longer rapping. They needed all their concentration and energy for the steep, slippery, stony climb.

'Ohmygrass! What's that?' Jaycey didn't dare look up. A dark shadow passed over them and slid silently away. Were the crows back? Huge ones this time? Crows big enough to eat Oxo in one go?

'Not a crow,' said Wills, a bit puzzled.

'That enormous mosquito, then?' whimpered Jaycey. 'The one we heard in the forest.'

'Too quiet for that,' said Wills.

'Was it the Lambad dude?' asked Links.

Sal didn't know. All her stomachs churned with fear. She racked her brains for some words of comfort from the Songs of the Fleece, but could find none.

'It was just a cloud,' said Wills. 'A long thin cloud.' But he didn't believe it himself.

The shaken Warriors shuffled closer together and continued climbing. They all had the feeling that they were being watched.

Luke forgot about the helicopter and warm prison cells as he hurried after Neil into the foothills. Neil's pace didn't slacken despite the awful conditions. He ploughed through the snowdrifts, sometimes knee deep, sometimes chest deep, his eyes blazing. He fell into holes and clambered quickly out again.

'This one smells of woolbags!' he shouted wildly, struggling out of a large hollow. 'We can't be far behind them. Go ahead, you stupid mutt,' he shouted at Saffron. 'Round 'em up.'

Saffron gave him a look and stuck close to Luke's side. They all scrambled, slipping and sliding over the icy rocks, and finally hoisted themselves on to the small flat area near the barn. Luke dropped to his knees in the snow, panting heavily.

'I can't go on!' he gasped. He was sweating from the exertion but the sweat was freezing on his face. 'I'm done for . . .'

Neil was looking briskly around. The grease spots had disappeared but their hoof prints were clearly visible, heading towards the barn.

'Ah ha!' he cried, hauling Luke to his feet. 'We've got them *trapped*!'

Again? Luke wondered how many times he'd heard that one but he didn't have the energy to argue.

Neil ran on, then stopped in front of the barn. The hoofprints didn't go in as he'd expected. They went round the side. He put a finger to his lips.

'They're trying to be clever,' he whispered. 'Making out they didn't go inside. But they don't get *me* that easily. Stand back.' And he barged the door with his shoulder.

It was a very large barn with wide double doors, neither of which moved.

'Yeah, well.' Neil lifted the long wooden latch instead and pushed.

The door swung quietly open and they stood on the threshold, peering in. The barn smelt of wool and petrol and hay. Daylight filtered through a dirty window.

'Close the door so they can't escape,' ordered Neil.

Luke did as he was told and they had to wait a moment until their eyes adjusted again.

'They're not here,' said Luke.

'Who said they were?' asked Neil angrily. Then he grabbed Luke's arm. 'But how handy is that?'

Luke peered and saw two quad bikes, parked near the opposite wall. Neil hurried towards them. He was suddenly jubilant.

'Some shepherds use quad bikes to round up their sheep,' he said, as if he knew all about it. 'Hop on.'

But as he swung into the saddle, a figure stepped out from behind the hay bales in the corner of the barn. His Very Nasty Boss.

Better known as Lady Caroline Babcott.

19
Bony Peak

Tod and Ida were shocked rigid. They had followed
Lady Babcott into the barn, looking for the sheep,
then they had all hidden behind the hay bales when
the men arrived. But as Lady Babcott stepped out
and showed herself, the kind smile they were used
to disappeared. She clearly knew one of the men and
he was afraid of her. He was shaking inside his filthy,
torn parka.

'It's all Luke's fault,' he gabbled. 'It was him who
chucked the phone out of the balloon basket. It was
him who . . .'

'Neil.'

'Yes, Lady B.'

'Shut up.'

'Yes, Lady B.'

'I didn't become very rich by listening to excuses.'

'No, Lady B.'

'And I don't intend to go to prison for the mistakes of a couple of bungling lightweights. What are you, Neil?'

'A couple of bungling lightweights, Lady B.'

'Exactly. Which is why I'm here in person. *You* may have been outwitted by a bunch of sheep; *I* shall not be. This is Tod and Ida, devoted owners of the mangy woolbags. *They* will retrieve the phone for us.'

She turned and smiled at Tod and Ida in her new cruel way.

'Won't you, dears?' she said sweetly. Then the smile snapped shut. 'Let's go.'

She swiftly mounted a quad bike. 'On this one with me, please, Ida. Tod, go with Neil.'

Tod didn't move. He glared at Lady Babcott, feeling betrayed but defiant.

'Why should I?' he eventually said.

'Because you want to see your sheep again,' said Lady Babcott. 'Alive.' Then she looked sharply at her bungling lightweight. 'You *can* drive one of these?'

'Oh, sure, sure,' said Neil quickly.

'Open the doors, geek,' ordered Lady Babcott.

171

Luke scurried to obey. Lady Babcott's quad bike blasted into life. The noise terrified Saffron, who yelped and darted out of the door with her tail between her legs. Neil fiddled with the controls on his bike but when nothing happened, Lady Babcott gave him a pitying look, leant over and started it for him.

'Hold on tight, kid!' snarled Neil at Tod, who had climbed on reluctantly behind him. 'I don't hang around.'

He didn't. He reversed rapidly into the hay bales, drove forward into a wall, then finally shot backwards out of the door.

'You're with us, geek,' Lady Babcott told Luke.

She drove out after Neil. Luke clung on desperately behind Ida as the bike accelerated up the icy path.

'It's all right, dear,' Ida assured him. 'I won't let you fall off.'

Luke felt more awful than ever. He would never be able to get her money back for her now, and here she was being kind to him.

The Warriors had climbed beyond the snow, up where the air was thin, clear and bitterly cold. Every few moments, a drifting icy mist enveloped them, then floated on. The path became narrower still, with a wall of slippery rock on one side and nothing on the other except a long drop to certain death.

They climbed head to rump, supporting one another as they sought each foothold, with Oxo as anchor ram at the rear, bracing himself and heaving his shoulders to help the stack of Warriors ever upwards.

Sal was beginning to weaken but she was determined not to fail. They must be close to the summit now. Desperately, she tried to inspire herself by chanting the Songs of the Fleece.

'High above the clouds, in the pasture of Great Aries . . .'

It came out as a gasp, but to her surprise, the immortal words were taken up behind her, by Links. Sort of.

'Where all sweet sheeps will graze, man,
An' there ain't no fence or boundaries . . .'
Then by Wills.
'The wise and ancient Soay lies
Upon his Unspun Fleece . . .'
Even Jaycey.

'And there is – ohmygrass! What was that!'

The long dark shadow that had passed over them on the lower slopes loomed again. A sense of foreboding flooded over them too. Some new terror was about to strike. They all felt it. Surely this time it *was* Lambad! Only Wills risked glancing up and losing his hoofhold. What he saw made his blood run cold. Floating not far above their heads was a long, black, narrow machine with wings. The worst thing about it was its absolute silence. It was a glider, though Wills didn't know that. And it was Top Secret, like the building on the summit of Bony Peak from which it had emerged. The building Kraw had warned them about. The building that was the headquarters of British Alien Research Military Intelligence. (BARMI for short.)

In the glider sat a grim-faced pilot in military uniform, two equally grim-faced observers also in military uniform, Nisha Patel and Tony Catchpole.

Tony wasn't grim-faced at all. He was very excited. A lot had happened to him since he'd left the sheep in the trailer and run off to Loch Glooming to meet Nisha.

The most exciting thing was that Nisha had been

174

waiting for him, and had seemed really pleased with the thistle he'd picked for her because he couldn't find any daffodils.

The second exciting thing was that he'd been taken seriously.

As he'd gabbled away to Nisha in the little café near the station, two men had sidled up and joined them. They offered to buy Tony a cup of tea. They had seen him on television talking about the sheep he'd witnessed being abducted by aliens. They believed in aliens.

'Do you know why the sheep have come here?' they asked.

Tony didn't.

'Do you know where they are now?'

Tony did. They were in the trailer where he had left them. Except that when they got back to the trailer, the sheep weren't there, after all.

'Will you help us find and identify them?' asked the men.

It was an invitation Tony couldn't refuse. They told Nisha that she must come too. There were to be no more news broadcasts until the sheep were found.

'Why ever not?' asked Nisha, but the men remained silent in a Top Secret sort of way.

So here they were in the black glider. Nisha was not excited. She was worried.

Tony's face was pressed against the window beside her, peering down at the clambering sheep.

'Is that them?' asked one of the observers.

'Definitely, definitely,' replied Tony.

The observer spoke quickly into his radio.

'Black Dog to BARMI HQ. Target confirmed.'

'Target!' Tony turned, reacting to the word. He stared at the observer. 'Target?' he said again.

The observer merely nodded, grim-faced as ever.

The panting sheep had finally reached the top of Bony Peak, just as the sun was starting to set again. They'd spent a whole day climbing. They gathered close, recovering their breath, then gazed ahead. The huge dark shadow cast by the silent sinister machine still fell across them, but they tried to ignore it. Their eyes were fixed elsewhere.

The summit was not a sharp point as it had appeared from below, but a small rocky plateau, on the far side of which stood the humans' building, as grey and forbidding as the mountain itself. In front of this fortress was some grass. Not that even Oxo was interested in eating at this special moment: the moment they had striven for; the purpose of their quest; the reason they had risked their lives. For there before the Rare Breed Warriors stood an ancient Soay.

He wasn't at all what they had expected. He was small and brown and scruffy and his horns, though down-turned, were chipped and dirty grey, not golden. He blinked at the Warriors but said nothing.

'Aries . . .?' breathed Sal, her four stomachs merging into one great trembling wobble of awe.

The Soay didn't reply.

Sal heard a little cough behind her. It was Wills.

'Umm . . . Sal.'

Sal turned and as she did so she saw, dotted amongst the rocks, more Soays. Hundreds of them. There were Soays everywhere. And lots of them looked old.

'Which one is Aries?' asked Wills.

Sal didn't know. She stared around, confused, panic rising inside her.

'These is just sheeply sheep, innit,' said Links, at last. 'Way too small to be the Golden Horn Dude.'

'Way too small,' agreed Oxo.

There was an uncomfortable silence, then Sal spoke again.

'Look over there . . .' Her voice was hushed.

The others followed her gaze. In the grass, close to the human fortress, was a large hollow in the ground.

'Of course!' Sal cried in relief. 'We won't actually *see* Lord Aries. We are not worthy to look upon him. But that sheep-shaped hollow is surely the resting place of the Ram of Rams . . .' She turned quickly to the others. 'We'll place the Baaton there for him. Don't be frightened, Jaycey dear. Come forward . . .'

'Ohmygrass . . . He won't come back and sit on me, will he?' whimpered Jaycey.

'No, dear. Sitting on you is not in the prophecy. Quickly now.'

'Um,' pointed out Wills anxiously, 'Kraw did say the human building was a bad place . . .'

But nobody was listening to him, least of all Sal. Even the circling black shadow that might be Lambad was shut from her mind. They were in the right place and they were in time. The prophecy was about to be fulfilled. She urged Jaycey and the Baaton towards the hollow.

The others followed, but as they did so, they heard a roar behind them. The roar of engines. Turning in alarm, they saw humans on quad bikes charging up the steep path towards them: the two men who'd been chasing them, a woman they didn't recognise . . . and Tod and Ida.

The quad bikes surged towards the sheep, then suddenly veered away, as if they were going to drive straight off the top of the mountain. Instead, they skidded to a halt at the last moment.

Tod's heart was thumping with fear as Lady Babcott leapt nimbly from her bike. To his horror, she dragged Ida with her and stood holding her at the very edge of the precipice.

'Right,' she said harshly to Tod. 'Get that phone from the sheep or your dear old granny goes for a walk in thin air.'

20
BARMI

Ida stayed very calm. Which is more than could be said for Tod.

'Gran!' he screamed, running towards her.

'I'm not bluffing,' warned Lady Babcott, and to prove it she gave Ida a little nudge. One of Ida's feet slipped off the edge. Lady Babcott let it dangle for a second, then dragged Ida back a fraction.

Luke gasped in horror but Neil didn't even blink. Lady B was ruthless. He was just glad it wasn't him she had hold of.

'Best do as she says,' he advised Tod.

Tod turned and raced, slipping and tripping, over the rocks towards the sheep.

He ran straight up to Jaycey and tried to grab the Baaton. Jaycey backed away and the others surrounded her protectively.

'Please!' cried Tod. 'Please let me have it.'

'Baaton . . . Baaton . . . Baaton . . .' bleated the Warriors.

Tod crouched in front of them and tried to explain.

'That lady wants the mobile phone,' he said, 'and if she doesn't get it, she's going to murder Gran.' He looked at Wills and pleaded. 'You understand, Wills. Can't you explain to the others? Please. Gran's going to die!'

Wills gazed at the sobbing boy, then turned to his fellow sheep.

'Warriors, the humans think the Baaton is just a mobile phone. They want it badly. So badly that Ida will be killed if we don't give it to them.'

'But we can't possibly give it to them!' gasped Sal. 'We brought it here to save Lord Aries. To save sheepdom from torment and death.'

'And we's only just in time, innit,' added Links.

Oxo and Jaycey nodded their heads in agreement. The black shadow had stopped passing over them but that didn't mean Lambad had gone. Maybe he had come down amongst the rocks. He could be anywhere.

Wills glanced across at Ida and the woman holding her.

'We can save Aries and thereby the whole of sheepkind,' he said. 'Or we can save Ida. There is only one Baaton. The choice is ours and we must make it now.'

The others turned to Sal.

'Your call,' Links said to her quietly.

Sal wished it wasn't. She looked at Wills, who gazed steadily back at her.

'Would Aries want Ida to die so he can live?' he asked. 'Aries, Ram of Rams, symbol of goodness?'

Sal's head was spinning. She gulped, then turned abruptly to Jaycey, mouthed up the plastic bag containing its precious Baaton, and dragged it roughly over Jaycey's head. She crossed slowly to Tod and dropped it at his feet.

'Thank you . . .' he said, but Sal had already turned away to hide her distress.

Tod understood that something was upsetting her dreadfully but he didn't have time to think about it. He grabbed up the plastic bag and turned back to his gran and Lady Babcott.

Lady Babcott smiled and moved away from the edge, though she didn't release her grip on Ida's bony arm.

'There!' she said to Neil. '*That's* how it's done.'

Tod began stumbling back over the rocks but the panic had subsided and his heart was thumping less loudly. He stopped and took the phone from the bag. Lady Babcott wasn't going to get it until his gran was safe.

Lady Babcott frowned, gripped Ida's arm more tightly and moved towards Tod, her other hand outstretched for the phone.

Tod didn't move. 'Not until you let Gran free,' he said.

Lady Babcott came a little closer. Then closer still. Tod put the phone behind his back. 'Let her go!' he demanded.

Lady Babcott snorted, released her grip on Gran's arm and gave her a little shove. Tod held out the phone again but as Lady Babcott's fingers curled to grasp it, she and Tod were both blinded by the beam of a huge searchlight. It swept backwards and forwards across the small plateau and a voice boomed through a megaphone.

'Drop that! And move away from the sheep at once! All of you.'

Tod turned and saw heavily armed soldiers in camouflage uniforms running towards them from the fortress. The megaphone boomed again.

'I said drop it!'

Lady Babcott dropped the phone.

'Over by the wall. All of you!'

The soldiers quickly surrounded Tod, Ida and Lady Babcott and began driving them towards the fortress. Other soldiers were driving Luke and Neil towards it too.

'Don't you know this is a top-secret establishment!' shouted an officer as they stumbled across the grass.

'If they did, sir,' pointed out a sergeant, 'it wouldn't be top secret.'

'Quite right, quite right. Move it, move it!'

Just in front of the fortress, there was a great wall of sandbags. The kind of thing soldiers shelter behind when there's going to be an explosion.

'Through there. Double quick!' The officer ushered them behind the sandbag wall.

To Tod and Ida's astonishment, Tony Catchpole and Nisha were already there.

'I'm ever so sorry, Ida,' Tony whispered, as the newcomers were herded in.

'What for?' Ida asked. She noticed that Nisha was wearing her cream suit again, which was asking for trouble on a mountain-top full of sheep.

'For identifying them from the glider,' said Tony. 'As the sheep the aliens abducted.'

'They can't believe in that nonsense, Tony dear,' smiled Ida.

'But they do.' Tony was almost weeping. 'They think your sheep are acting as spies for aliens. They think the thing Jaycey's been carrying round her neck is a transmitter sending information back to the spaceship: information about their top-secret headquarters. They're BARMI, you see.'

Ida didn't see. Neither did any of the others.

'So why have they made us all come behind here?' asked Tod.

Tony swallowed hard. 'They say the sheep have got to be destroyed before they can pass on any more secret information.'

'No!' Ida grabbed Tony's arm. 'Tell them they're wrong. Tell them they're mad.'

'I have,' said Tony miserably. 'But they won't listen. They're preparing the explosives now. They're going to blow your sheep up!'

Tod put his arm around Gran's shoulder. Tony put his arm around Nisha's. Luke sniffed and used the sleeve of Neil's jacket to wipe tears from his eyes. He didn't even notice the smell. Only Neil and Lady Babcott were unaffected. In fact, they were delighted.

'You're a lucky lightweight,' Lady Babcott told Neil. 'The mobile's going to be blown to smithereens. Bang! End of all your problems.'

Neil risked a reply. 'All *our* problems, Lady B. All *our* problems.' And he grinned back. 'Cheers!'

Out in the grassy, sheep-shaped hollow, the Warriors were confused by the searchlight and the megaphone, and all the human comings and goings. Wills had no idea what was happening, but he felt very uneasy, even though Ida seemed to be safe now.

The Baaton lay face down on the grass, a little way off, where Lady Babcott had dropped it. Delight and relief surged through Sal's stomachs: Aries' power would be restored after all!

'We should move it, innit?' said Links. 'Turn it up the right way for the Golden Horn Dude.'

He stepped helpfully towards the Baaton, then stopped. Something else peculiar and scary was happening.

'Ohmygrass . . .' Jaycey had seen it too. 'Ohmygrass, a giant creepy-crawly . . .'

They watched in horror as a thing the size of a new-born lamb but with legs like a spider crawled slowly from the humans' building towards them. It was made of hard, grey metal and instead of eyes it had antennae sticking from the top of its head.

The humans behind the sandbag barrier were watching it as well.

'It's a robot,' said Tony grimly. 'And it'll be carrying enough explosives to send all your poor sheep sky high.'

'No!' yelled Tod, and he tried to scramble out over the wall of sandbags. But Gran pulled him back again.

'It's no good, Tod,' she sobbed.

'How do they control it?' asked Luke, though he had already guessed the answer.

'With a computer,' said Tony. 'It's in that tent along there.'

Luke peered to his left and saw a small tent tucked safely behind the sandbags. The soldiers who were supposed to be guarding them were now peering in through the flap of the tent. They were too interested in what was happening inside it to notice what was happening outside.

'Sheep lady,' Luke whispered. 'Come with me. You and the boy.'

Tod and Ida looked at him suspiciously, but he'd already turned and was creeping towards the tent. They followed cautiously. When they were close, Luke whispered again.

'Create a distraction. Get the guards out of the way.'

Tod cottoned on quickly.

'I can't take any more!' he suddenly wailed. 'I'd rather die with our sheep!' And he climbed nimbly on to the sandbag wall. Gran clambered creakily up after him.

'Yes!' she yelled. 'Blow us up too! Goodbye, Planet Earth . . .'

The soldiers jerked their heads from inside the

tent and raced towards the old lady and the boy now standing on top of the sandbags.

'Get down!' they ordered as they ran. But Tod and Ida dodged along the sandbag wall, wailing and yelling, flailing their arms wildly and kicking at the soldiers trying to drag them off.

Luke slipped inside the tent. In front of him was the computer and in front of that, concentrating hard, was a uniformed soldier. Luke stopped. He didn't know what to do next. He supposed he should creep up and strangle the soldier and take over the keyboard. But he couldn't bring himself to do that. As he dithered, the soldier suddenly sat up straight. He coughed, retched and clasped a hand over his mouth.

'Ughhh! What's that stench?' he gasped. His chair toppled backwards as he stood up and blundered to the tent flap, overwhelmed in the confined space by a toxic mix of manure, wet dog and llama spit coming from the jacket Luke was wearing.

'I'm gonna throw up . . .' Hand over his mouth, he shoved Luke aside without seeing who he was and charged out. 'Take over, mate . . .' he groaned as he ran.

Luke didn't need telling twice.

He didn't bother to pick up the chair. He knelt in front of the keyboard and began dabbing at it furiously. On screen, the robot was now closing in on the sheep. Luke keyed in numbers and letters as quickly as he could. The sheep were backing away from the robot but much too slowly. Luke broke out into a cold sweat and dabbed harder. Outside, he heard the sergeant begin the countdown.

'Ten . . . nine . . . eight . . .'

Luke tried to concentrate. He could do this – he could stop the robot – if he only had time . . . The sheep, led by the skinny lamb, finally turned and ran. But not fast enough. Nor far enough.

'Seven . . . six . . . five . . .'

Luke took a deep breath and did what a geek never, ever does. He pulled all the plugs. He saw the robot spin around in a confused figure of eight, then the screen went blank.

The explosion was massive.

21
Tod's Surprise

The Warriors watched, crowded together at the mouth of the cave to which Wills had been trying to lead them. He'd noticed it just before the quad bikes had arrived and wondered if it might come in useful. They'd reached it just in time. They flinched at the bangs and whizzes, but marvelled at the bright flashes amid the billowing smoke. And when the final boom shook the rocks, and the smoke cleared a little, they saw that the Baaton had gone.

'Ohmygrass . . .' said Jaycey. 'Was that Aries taking the Baaton back?'

'Taking it back, regaining his strength and challenging Lambad all at once . . .' breathed Sal.

'Butting his butt big time,' said Oxo.

'The Golden Horn Dude's back in charge, innit?' said Links.

'Ohmygrass . . . Look . . .' gasped Jaycey.

The Warriors gazed upwards. Above the mountain, the smoke had formed itself into a great cloud, a cloud that nobody could deny was shaped like a sheep. It floated, majestic and free, then gradually dissolved in the pale evening sky to reveal the brightest star the Rare Breeds had ever seen.

'Aries . . .'

It was not only Sal who felt the presence of the Sheep of Sheep. Every Warrior experienced the same deep glow.

'Job done, man,' said Links. 'Job done . . .'

There had never been a better time for high hooves all round.

'Any ideas what went wrong?' asked the officer.

'No, sir,' said the soldiers, who had succeeded in getting Tod and Ida off the wall just before the explosion. They didn't want to admit that they hadn't been guarding the tent properly.

'No, sir,' said the soldier who'd left his computer to be sick. He didn't want to admit that he'd allowed a maniac in a stinking jacket to pull all the plugs.

'Well . . . No harm done,' said the officer. 'Didn't go off exactly as planned but the objective has been achieved. No sign of the modified sheep or their equipment. Totally vaporised.' He smiled and dismissed the soldiers. 'Showed those aliens a thing or two, eh, chaps!'

A little later, the sergeant drove the civilians back down to the quad bike barn.

'Don't tell anyone we're BARMI up here,' he barked as he drove off into the darkness again.

Ida, who had kept her tears in check until now, could contain them no longer.

'Our poor sheep,' she sobbed. 'Blown to bits . . . They didn't deserve that, did they, Tod?'

Tod did his best to comfort his gran. And Nisha did the same for Tony, who tried not to enjoy her being nice to him, because he was upset, as it was all his fault in the first place.

Luke kept quiet. He didn't understand what had happened. He was sure he'd seen the robot zoom away from the sheep at the last moment.

Neil and Lady Babcott looked at them all and laughed loudly.

'Losers!' sneered Neil.

Up on Bony Peak, all was now peaceful, but Wills was anxious to get away from the strange humans in their scary fortress.

'Shall we go home?' he suggested, leading the way out of the cave.

A brilliant moon had risen to join the bright star. The night air was still and very cold. The path they had climbed up so laboriously was now a smooth slope of ice, disappearing down the mountainside.

The Warriors blinked at it for a few moments, all sharing the same thought.

'Who's going first?' asked Oxo. Then he answered his own question by jumping on and slithering away downhill with a great exultant shout.

'Five for one and all for five!'

One by one, the others followed.

'Ohmygrassohmygrassohmygrass . . .!'

'Cool runnins, dudes . . .!'

'Aries for ever . . .!'

'Eppingham here we come!'

They landed on top of each other in a woolly heap

at the bottom of the ice slide. They were aware of the barn, and humans, then of squeals of disbelief and delight. And then a thousand-year-old granny hurled herself on top of them, followed by Tod, the boy who brought them cauliflowers some nights. Tony and Nisha were holding hands and cheering.

Luke used the stinking jacket sleeve to wipe away his own tears of relief.

'You can keep the jacket, if you like, Supergeek.'

Luke turned. Neil was grinning at him.

'You can have your parka back too. I won't be needing it. We're off.'

'Off?'

'Me and Lady B. Back to London in the chopper. Then it's first class to somewhere exotic where the only ice is in the drinks.'

'What about me?'

'What about you? Those nice guys with the bombs have blown your mobile with the you-know-what into tiny little bits. You've got nothing more to worry about, mate.'

'No . . .' said Luke. It slowly dawned on him that he was free of Neil at last. He still had plenty to worry about, in fact, like how to get home, but the biggest worry of all was about to disappear from his life.

'Right,' he said. 'See you, then.'

'Unlikely,' laughed Neil, and he sauntered round the side of the barn and out of sight.

Tod and Ida had forgotten about the helicopter, and neither Tony nor Nisha had realised it was there. The sudden noise as its engine roared into life cut short their joyful reunion with the flock. They all stared as it rose from behind the barn, hovered for a moment, then banked rapidly away to the south. Lady Babcott, they could see, was skilfully at the controls. Neil was waving and laughing down at them.

'Bye, suckers!' he mouthed.

When the noise had died away and the helicopter was only a speck disappearing into the moonlight, they all suddenly felt very flat and down again. And very cold.

'Well,' said Ida, leading the way into the barn. 'That Neil's right, I suppose. It's the last we'll see of them. Or our money.'

The others followed, glad to get out of the night air. Luke took the stinking jacket off and dropped it outside. He didn't want to upset any more stomachs. Tony found a switch, and a neon strip hanging from the rafters flickered, then filled the barn with harsh white light.

'It's all my fault,' he said miserably to Ida. 'If I hadn't thought I'd seen a UFO abducting your sheep, those BARMI blokes wouldn't have tried to blow them up. Then we'd still have the evidence.'

'It's not your fault, it's mine,' said Luke, even more miserably. 'I should have guessed Neil was up to something when he bet I couldn't download bank data on to my phone.'

Ida patted him on the shoulder.

'Well, so long as you didn't mean to steal from us, dear, we won't hold it against you.'

Luke felt even worse. 'They're crooks, cheats, swindlers!' he said angrily. 'And they're going to get away with it!'

'I don't think so.'

Everyone turned to stare at Tod.

'In fact,' he said, 'I'm sure they're not.' And from

197

his pocket he took a small square of plastic.

'The SIM card!' yelled Luke. 'You've got the SIM card from my phone!'

'I took it out before I gave the phone to Lady B,' Tod said. 'Once I knew she wasn't going to shove you over the edge of the mountain, of course, Gran.'

'All the bank details are on that tiny card?' asked Tony.

Luke nodded. 'It'll also prove that Neil transferred them to his computer. And *that* will prove how he transferred the money on to Lady B.'

Ida stood back, beaming at her grandson for a moment, then threw her arms around him in a rib-crushing hug.

'What a boy!' she yelled. 'What a boy!'

Tod blushed scarlet. Tony punched the air and jumped up and down, laughing. Nisha laughed too and tucked the thistle Tony had picked for her more firmly into her hair.

The sheep watched with interest. Humans could be very peculiar sometimes. Then they remembered that they hadn't eaten since . . . they couldn't remember since when. Oxo headed for the hay bales in the corner, then stopped suddenly. He sniffed. There was a smell in the barn he didn't like. Then he heard a noise he didn't like. Dog! Saffron slunk out from behind the hay bales, tail still between her legs, whimpering softly.

'Saffron! I thought I'd lost you! Here, girl . . . It's all right . . .' Luke held out his arms and the dog instantly perked up. Her tail started wagging, the whimpers changed to short, excited little barks, and she hurled herself at the human she had come to regard as her own. The Warriors huddled together anxiously for a moment, but it was clear that this sheepdog was no longer interested in sheep.

Tod cut the string around some of the hay bales and the Warriors got stuck in. Oxo even ate the string.

When Tod went back and sat with the other humans, he suddenly looked worried.

'I'm sorry, Luke,' he said. 'I think when we give the SIM card to the police, they'll arrest you too. You'll probably go to prison.'

Luke shrugged. 'I deserve it,' he said, 'for being so stupid.'

'No you don't,' said Ida. 'We'll speak up for you.

And you're not stupid. Just a bit gullible, that's all. And there's plenty of that about,' she added, with a little smile that Tony didn't notice.

Luke smiled too. He hoped she was right. About prison. And about not being stupid.

'But the bank won't want you back,' continued Ida. 'So you'll have to find another job.' She thought for a moment. 'You're good with technology. My hens would probably like some video footage to go with their egg-laying music. D'you think you could manage that?'

Luke blinked.

'And then there's Wills. He's an exceptionally bright lamb. I'm sure he'd like to become computer literate.'

Luke looked across at the small brown sheep, chomping hay, then wiped a tear of gratitude away with the corner of his T-shirt.

'That should keep you going for a couple of months,' said Ida. 'Till you get yourself straight again.' She paused. 'And you can bring your non-sheepdog, if you like.'

Luke needed all his T-shirt for tears after that.

Nisha was busy dabbing at her mobile phone. She called the police. And then Organic TV, but only about Neil and Lady B. She didn't mention the sheep. 'They've been exposed to enough media attention,' she said. 'They deserve some peace. You all do.'

Tony decided he loved her even more. He found another thistle amongst the hay. It was brown and prickly but Nisha put it in her hair with the other one just the same.

'Oh,' she added with a mischievous smile, 'and I've arranged some transport home.'

22
Up and Away

The dramatic arrest of Neil and Lady Babcott, when they stepped from the helicopter on to the roof of her house back in London, was the main news on television that night.

At Loch Glooming, Tony's Cousin Angus nodded wisely as he slurped his evening porridge and watched the news.

'I knew wee Tony was up tae something,' he told his cat. 'He's nae as daft as he looks.' Next morning, he and his cat had something else to talk about: a huge golden hot-air balloon was being inflated in the station car park.

Tony just stood and stared when he saw it. On the long walk back down from the mountains, he'd been wondering what sort of transport Nisha had arranged but never guessed it would be a balloon.

'No aliens,' she said, teasing. 'I promise.'

The pilot had thoughtfully provided a ramp for the sheep to climb up. Oxo was dubious.

'Will there be in-flight snacks?' he asked Wills.

Then he glimpsed a large picnic hamper in one corner and trotted eagerly on board. The other sheep followed him, then Saffron and all the humans. It was a bit of a squash but nobody minded. Luke blushed and hid his face when the pilot explained, very clearly, that nothing, but nothing, must be dropped over the side. Not ever.

The gas burner roared and the great balloon rose into the sky.

'Bye, Angus,' yelled Tony. 'Sorry about the manure!'

The Rare Breed Warriors peered down at the balloon's shadow, drifting harmlessly across the ground below. They raised their heads to the now distant mountain. The sheep-shaped cloud had long since vanished. The star had faded too now, in the bright sunshine. All was well.

'We's the Eppingham Posse
And our mission is complete,
Cos the Golden Horn Dude
Is back on his feet.
Our shinin' star's back
And the darkness all gone.
Aries got the Baaton,
And now we's goin' home.
We finally done the business
An' our satisfaction's deep.
We chew a lot of cud, man,
Cos we's the Warrior Sheep.'

Join the Rare Breed sheep
on their next baaarmy quest!

The Warrior SHEEP

Go West

Turn the page to read the first chapter . . .

1
Red Tongue

They only went into the barn to get out of the rain. But that just goes to show that big adventures can start when you least expect them.

Sheep, even Rare Breed sheep, don't normally mind getting wet but it had been pouring for days and the paddock was hoof deep in mud. Jaycey, the pretty little Jacob, had had enough.

'Ohmygrass . . .' she said, trotting into the cosy barn. 'All this rain. I'm having such a bad hair day.'

'Don't be silly, dear,' said Sal, the fat and motherly Southdown ewe as she followed. 'Only humans have hair. And there's no such thing as a bad *fleece* day.'

'That's right, man,' agreed Links, the large Lincoln Longwool ram, even though his own woolly locks were dangling damply in front of his eyes and he couldn't see where he was going. 'Fleece is cool, innit.'

He bumped into the doorpost on his way in.

Wills, the skinny Welsh Balwin lamb, skipped in after Links. He liked the barn. Usually, there was a laptop in there.

Only Oxo, the great Oxford ram, was reluctant to go inside. The rain made the grass grow longer and sweeter. What was there not to like about that? But he was a sheep and sheep stick together, so he tugged up a last juicy mouthful and squeezed in after the rest.

The hens, who lived in the barn, squawked and fluttered for a few minutes then settled again and the sheep made themselves comfortable on the straw covered floor. They sat facing the laptop, which was propped on a bale of hay in the middle of the barn. Jaycey and Wills, the smallest, were at the front, with Sal, Oxo and Links behind.

The laptop belonged to Ida White, who owned Eppingham Farm where the Rare Breed sheep lived. She often left it in the barn playing music for the hens. This particular wet spring day she was downloading some new tunes for them, some gentle pieces as a change from their usual pop and rock. The second track was just beginning as the sheep settled down.

Wills, whose mother had died when he was young, had spent his early lambhood with Ida and her grandson, Tod, in the farmhouse kitchen. He had learned a lot about human ways and could even read a little. He slowly read out the words on the screen.

'Sheep May Safely Graze . . . J. S. Bach.'

'What's J.S. Bach?' asked Oxo, hopefully. 'Something you can graze on?'

Wills shook his head. 'No. I think it's the name of the composer. The man who wrote the music.'

'Shhh,' said Sal. She was gazing happily at the laptop. As the music played, the screen showed a picture of sheep grazing in a beautiful sunlit valley. 'How fortunate we are to be sheep,' she murmured.

'Yeah,' agreed Links. 'But this ain't exactly a banging vibe, is it?' His curls bobbed up and down as he nodded his head, trying to compose a rap. It wasn't easy to make the words fit the slow music.

'We is Ovis Aries, that's our Latin name,

But you can call us sheep cos it means the same . . .'

Jaycey was also peering at the laptop but she wasn't interested in the music or the pictures. She'd noticed

209

her own reflection in the screen and was studying it carefully. Finally, she relaxed. Not a bad hair day after all. And she was massively prettier than any of the safely grazing sheep on the screen.

Oxo tried listening to the music for a few seconds but could only hear his own stomachs rumbling so he gave up and dozed off.

Then it happened.

The sheep on the screen disappeared and, from the blackness that replaced them, a red tongue emerged. It filled the screen, showing the rough, red surface and the tonsils dangling behind. Then came the voice.

'Hi, all you Rams and Ewes and Lambs. This message is for *you*. We're gonna slaughter you. We're on our way. Red Tongue! Remember the name!'

The sheep scrambled to their hooves and looked fearfully around. Oxo marched bravely to the doorway and glared out. The paddock was empty.

The laptop spoke again. 'Red Tongue! Remember the name!' Then the tongue disappeared and the sunlit valley was back again.

'Ohmygrass . . .' Jaycey huddled close to Sal. 'What was that?'

'I think,' said Wills, 'it was a pop-up.'

'What's a pop-up?' asked Oxo.

'A sort of advertisement,' said Wills, though he didn't really know what an advertisement was.

Oxo lowered his great head and pawed the barn floor with a hoof. 'Just let him pop up again,' he snorted. 'I'll be ready next time.'

Sal raised a hoof for silence. 'Red Tongue . . .? Red Tongue . . .?' She was speaking in the odd voice she used when she was trying to remember something important. 'Yes . . .' she said at last. 'It's there in the Songs of the Fleece!'

'Uh-oh . . .' murmured Links warily.

The Songs of the Fleece were ancient. They had been handed down from ewe to lamb for centuries. Not many sheep knew all 365 verses like Sal did, but most knew a few. Sal looked gravely at her fellow Rare Breeds.

'Verse 204,' she announced. 'One of the prophetic verses.' Then she added for Wills' sake, 'Most of the Songs tell of our glorious history, you see, dear. The prophetic verses tell us what is to come.'

Wills nodded politely. Despite not having had a

mother to teach him sheeply things, he knew that much. He glanced at the laptop again. He felt sure he'd heard Ida say pop-ups were a nuisance. They arrived from nowhere then disappeared again. Just like the red tongue had done.

But Sal was clearing her throat so Wills turned to listen.

'A terrible monster will come from the West,' she cried dramatically,

'And a brave flock of Warriors will be put to the test.

For this monster has woken from centuries of sleep,

And its stomach will hunger for sheep. Then more sheep.

Hundreds of thousands will die every hour,

All the sheep in the world it will seek to devour.'

Sal paused for breath but before she could start again, Jaycey's trembling voice had taken up the verse.

'Like a gigantic dog from the West it will come . . .

And the name of this monster, be warned, is: Red Tongue.'

Jaycey looked at them all with frightened eyes. 'My Mum taught me that.'

She wobbled on her dainty feet then fainted.

There was silence for a few moments then Links said, 'So. We's done for, is it? We's all gonna be eaten by a monster dog.'

'The Songs of the Fleece are never wrong,' said Sal.

Oxo frowned. 'Yeah but what was that about Warriors?'

Jaycey opened one eye. 'They'll be put to the test,' she wailed. 'I don't want to be put to the test.'

There was another silence while they all pondered.

'Is it us again, Sal?' asked Wills.

Once before, the little flock of Rare Breed sheep from Eppingham Farm had been called by the Songs of the Fleece to save sheepdom. They had destroyed Lambad the Bad and saved Lord Aries, the mighty Ram of Rams who lives above the clouds.

Sal answered Wills' question by reciting the next two lines.

'Who will come forward in the hour of need?
Hope will lie only with those of Rare Breed.'

Oxo turned towards the doorway. 'Can't be clearer than that,' he said. 'Let's go!' and he charged out.

'Yeah, man', agreed Links. 'The Eppingham Rare Breeds is the rarest of the rare, innit.'

'We did it once, we *can* do it again,' agreed Wills bravely.

But then Oxo reappeared. 'So, um, where does this Red Tongue hang out, exactly?' he asked.

Sal thought hard then cleared her throat again.

'To the place where the monster first wakes you must go,

Where the sun scorches fleeces and the hottest winds blow.

But only the bravest will withstand this test.

Remember. Red Tongue . . . will wake in the *West*!'

She dropped her head, briefly overwhelmed by the task facing them. The discomforts and dangers of their first quest came back to her. They came back to all the sheep. Was it really possible to survive and triumph a second time? And where was the *West*, anyway?

Wills ran through the verse in his head. They had to go West, to a place where the hottest winds blow . . . Not Wales then, he thought. He had been born in

West Wales and didn't remember any hot winds there. No, it had to be somewhere much further away than Wales. He tried to picture the maps in Tod's atlas. West . . . Very hot . . . He realized the others were looking at him expectantly and tried to sound more confident than he felt.

'The most likely place,' he announced, 'is America.'

'No problem,' said Oxo and turned once more towards the barn door.

'Uh, there is actually,' said Wills. 'America's across the sea. How will we get there?'

'We are sheep!' declared Sal. 'Famed as great thinkers. Think, all of you. Think.'

So they thought and they were thinking so hard they didn't hear a car drive slowly along the lane and pull up outside the farmhouse.

The smartly-dressed driver leaned from the car window and wrinkled his nose.

'Ugh!' he said. 'The country!'

He straightened his tie, picked up his briefcase and stepped out, placing his shiny shoes in the mud. He had an important message for Mrs Ida White. He had better deliver it.

Christopher Russell was a postman when he had his first radio play broadcast in 1975, having given up a job in the civil service to do shift work and have more daytime hours for writing. Since 1980, he has been a full-time television and radio scriptwriter, and, more recently, a children's novelist. His wife Christine has always been closely involved with his work, storylining and script editing, and has television credits of her own.

THE QUEST OF THE WARRIOR SHEEP is the first book they have written together.

EGMONT PRESS: ETHICAL PUBLISHING

Egmont Press is about turning writers into successful authors and children into passionate readers – producing books that enrich and entertain. As a responsible children's publisher, we go even further, considering the world in which our consumers are growing up.

Safety First
Naturally, all of our books meet legal safety requirements. But we go further than this; every book with play value is tested to the highest standards – if it fails, it's back to the drawing-board.

Made Fairly
We are working to ensure that the workers involved in our supply chain – the people that make our books – are treated with fairness and respect.

Responsible Forestry
We are committed to ensuring all our papers come from environmentally and socially responsible forest sources.

For more information, please visit our website at www.egmont.co.uk/ethical